# YOUR LOVE

# IS MINE

**The Maine Sullivans**

**Cassie Sullivan and Flynn Stewart**

Bella Andre

**YOUR LOVE IS MINE**

The Maine Sullivans

Cassie Sullivan and Flynn Stewart

© 2019 Bella Andre

**Sign up for Bella's New Release Newsletter**

www.BellaAndre.com/newsletter

**bella@bellaandre.com**

**www.BellaAndre.com**

**Bella on Twitter:** @bellaandre

**Bella on Facebook:** facebook.com/bellaandrefans

Flynn Stewart, an award-winning screenwriter, seems to have the perfect Hollywood life. Until his dark past comes crashing back when he learns his long-lost sister has passed away—and he has a six-month-old niece named Ruby. Flynn vows to give the little girl who now means everything to him a better childhood than he or his sister ever had. So when he finds out that Ruby's nanny is trying to sell their story to the press, he takes his niece as far from Hollywood as he can.

One of seven siblings in Bar Harbor, Maine, Cassie Sullivan has always been grateful for the love and support of her tight-knit family. Because of them, she had the courage to create a successful candy confection business. When a friend of her cousin needs a place to stay with his baby for a few weeks, she's happy to offer him her cabin in the woods. And from the moment she meets Flynn and Ruby, her heart is lost to the gorgeous man and his adorable little girl.

Flynn has never met anyone as cheerful and open as Cassie. Instantly drawn to her, he finds himself telling her things about his past that he's never spoken of to anyone—things that make him certain he could never be worthy of her. Only, Cassie isn't about to let the pair who have stolen her heart go without a fight—using all the light, love, and laughter she can them. Will the nightmares from Flynn's past continue to haunt him and steal away the joy of a future with Cassie? Or will Cassie's love, and the support of her big family, be powerful enough to help him face his long-buried demons and conquer them at last?

## A note from Bella

Welcome to the Maine branch of the Sullivan family!

*Your Love Is Mine* was an absolute joy to write, not only because I adore Cassie and Flynn as a couple, but also because I am beyond thrilled to finally get to write about Ethan Sullivan, his wife, Beth, and their seven children. I can't wait to watch sparks fly as each of the seven siblings falls in love!

If this is your first time reading about the Sullivans, you can easily read each book as a stand-alone—and there is a Sullivan family tree available on my website (www.bellaandre.com/sullivan-family-tree) so you can see how the books are connected!

Happy reading,
*Bella Andre*

P.S. More stories about the Maine Sullivans are coming soon! Please be sure to sign up for my newsletter (bellaandre.com/newsletter) so that you don't miss out on any new book announcements.

# CHAPTER ONE

"Oh my gosh, she's *gorgeous*."

The words spilled from Cassie's lips the moment she saw the man standing on the front porch of her cabin—and the baby he was holding.

Instinctively, Cassie reached out to stroke the baby's soft hair, the same way she might with her sister's and cousins' young children. But before she could make contact, the little girl buried her face in the man's neck and held on tight, while he gathered her closer, clearly intent on protecting her.

Feeling like she'd made a huge misstep within seconds of meeting her new tenants, Cassie dropped her arm to her side and stepped back. "You must be Flynn and Ruby. Come on in."

Slowly, Flynn walked inside the cabin, and she got the sense that he was assessing whether he wanted to stay or not. The baby lifted her head briefly at the sound of her name before burying it again in the crook of his neck.

"I'm Cassie. It's nice to meet you. How was your

trip? You must be exhausted from the flights and layovers and the drive from the airport."

Ruby rubbed her eyes as though she was ready for a nap. Though Flynn looked like he could use one too, he simply replied, "We're fine."

"Great!" Cassie smiled at him even though she had a feeling any hope of an answering smile was slim to none. "I hope my cabin will work out for you. I've stocked the fridge. I wasn't sure about what kind of food Ruby eats, or if she's even on solids yet, so I got one jar of everything, from pureed carrots to peas to potatoes." When she was nervous, Cassie talked. A lot. Unfortunately, the fewer responses she got, the more she rambled to fill the empty space. "I also found a crib for you to use, along with a changing table and a few stuffed animals and a rubber ducky for the bath, plus some soft baby blankets and diapers in a range of sizes. The crib is set up in the master bedroom for now, but I can help you move it into the guest bedroom if that's where you'd rather have it."

"The master is fine."

There was that word again. *Fine.* Which, in her experience, usually meant anything but.

"Honestly," she told him, "I'd like to help. If you want to check out the cabin to see if there's anything else you need for tonight, or would like help moving things around, I can pitch in while I'm still here."

For a long moment, he simply stared at her. Almost like she was speaking a foreign language. Or, maybe, *all* foreign languages at once.

Finally, he nodded. "We'll be right back."

Once they had disappeared down the hall and into the master bedroom, Cassie let out a long breath. She'd made a fool of herself with all that inane chatter. If only she didn't feel so nervous.

Part of the problem was that she'd never known how to act around good-looking men she wasn't related to. It didn't help that Flynn Stewart took *good-looking* to another level entirely.

She knew who he was, of course. An award-winning screenwriter who had recently dated one of *People* magazine's "Most Beautiful" women, Flynn was nearly as famous as the actors who played the starring roles in his movies. But there was a big difference between seeing his photo online and meeting him in person.

Flynn was broader, bigger, and altogether more imposing live and in the flesh.

Since he was going to be living in her cabin for the next few weeks, it was high time to pull herself together and stop acting like a bumbling fool around him. So what if he was staggeringly good-looking? And brilliantly talented? She was simply offering him a place to stay, far from the glare of the Hollywood spotlight.

Cassie doubted the two of them would see much of each other once he and Ruby settled in.

Her heart softened as she thought about the sweet baby in Flynn's arms. Cassie's cousin Smith, who was one of the biggest movie stars in the world, had given her the bare bones of Flynn and Ruby's story. Evidently, one of Flynn's relatives had recently passed away, and he had adopted the little girl. Now, due to his fame, they needed to go somewhere remote and private to escape the endless camera flashes and questions from the paparazzi. Smith and Valentina had loved spending their honeymoon in Cassie's cabin earlier that year, so they'd immediately thought of it as a refuge for Flynn. Of course, any friend of Smith's was a friend of Cassie's, so she was more than happy to offer it.

She'd bought the cabin a few years back with the intention of renovating and flipping the run-down building set in the middle of a hundred wooded acres. But after she had put in the sweat equity of sanding and varnishing the floors, installing new kitchen cupboards, and painting each room the perfect color, she'd fallen too much in love with it to sell it. She was toying with the idea of leaving downtown Bar Harbor and living in it full time, but until it felt like the right time to make the leap, she was happy to lend it out to friends and family.

Flynn came back into the living room emptyhanded. "Ruby took one look at the crib and pretty much made a dive for it. She didn't sleep well on the plane." Looking utterly exhausted himself, he ran a hand over the heavy stubble on his chin. At a glance, he was rugged enough to be an outdoor adventurer, rather than someone who sat at a computer for hours on end spinning stories. "Thank you for everything you've done to set up your cabin for her." His voice was slightly gruff as he added, "For both of us."

"It's my pleasure." She smiled again, happy that she could help in some small way. She sincerely hoped they would be happy in this peaceful spot. "If there is anything else you need, just ask."

"There won't be."

She couldn't keep her eyebrows from rising at his definitive statement made in a rather gruff tone. "Okay." She backed toward the door. "I'll get out of your way." He remained silent while she grabbed her bag and car keys. "My phone number is on the counter." She didn't know what else there was to say. Especially when he wasn't adding anything into the mix. She opened the front door and stepped out onto the porch, feeling more awkward by the second. "Bye." She pulled the door closed behind her and headed to her car.

Sliding behind the wheel, she pulled out her phone

to text Smith: *Flynn and Ruby are here and settling in.*

His response was lightning fast: *Thanks again for letting them use your cabin. I know it will make a huge difference in their lives.*

Cassie sent back a smiley face: *Happy to help!*

And she truly was, even if Flynn obviously wanted to be left alone.

★ ★ ★

In his early twenties, Flynn had done an eighty-mile solo trek to Everest Base Camp wearing a fifty-pound backpack. He'd slept on the ground most nights and topped fifteen thousand feet in altitude.

Even then he couldn't remember feeling as tired as he did now. So exhausted that once he went into the bedroom to check on Ruby and sat in the armchair next to the crib, he could easily have closed his eyes and fallen asleep if he hadn't been so concerned about his niece waking up frightened in another strange bedroom.

Good thing he was used to surviving on little sleep. Until he was seventeen, he'd slept with one eye open, never sure what state his father would be in when he got home from the bar. After that, though he'd gotten away from his dad, Flynn still stayed awake at night, sure that it was only a matter of time before he was exposed as a lying fraud, certain that someone would surely realize *Flynn Stewart* was a character he had created out of thin air...and desperation.

Fifteen minutes after he'd settled Ruby in the crib, just as he'd expected, she woke up with a loud wail. By the time he reached in to pick her up, she was holding on to the bars like a little prisoner, tear tracks wet on her rosy cheeks.

"It's okay," he said softly. "I'm here."

She didn't smile as he picked her up, simply let out a jagged sigh of relief as he drew her close against him.

Catching sight of their reflection in a full-length mirror on the back of the door, he noted that this was how the two of them had been connected since he'd taken custody of her three weeks ago. Apart from Ruby's sporadic naps, and when she settled into her crib for, at best, six hours each night, he was tethered to his six-month-old niece around the clock.

She was the only person on earth who truly mattered to him...even though he hadn't known she existed three weeks ago.

# CHAPTER TWO

*Three weeks earlier...*

Flynn didn't recognize the number of the caller who had been trying to reach him for the past hour. He always turned his phone to do-not-disturb mode while he wrote, to minimize distractions, so he hadn't realized anyone had been calling until he took his first break. After a handful of brushes with the paparazzi a few years back, he no longer accepted voice mail from numbers that weren't in his contacts list.

As he stared at the area code from the town where he'd grown up, his chest tightened. Had it finally happened? Had someone put two and two together and realized that Flynn Stewart wasn't who he claimed to be?

He'd run from his past for nearly two decades, but he'd always known he wouldn't be able to run forever. No one could—not even a man who was a master at creating fictional stories that seemed more true than real life.

Flynn closed his laptop on his screenplay in progress and took a deep breath before hitting the redial button. Only, when the woman with the cigarette-worn voice began speaking, there was no relief in realizing she wasn't calling to expose him—she didn't even know his name, calling him Fred instead of Flynn. Instead, what she told him stunned him speechless.

His long-lost sister had not only died of an overdose, she'd also given birth to a daughter a little more than five months before.

Grief and guilt pummeled him, harder than any of his father's blows ever had.

All his life, Flynn had tried to protect his sister from their parents. When Flynn had left for Los Angeles at seventeen, he'd begged Sarah to come with him. But at sixteen, she'd already been lost to him, deep-diving into the same world of drugs and alcohol as their parents.

A year later—after their father had died in jail, with their mother subsequently drinking herself into an early grave—Flynn went back to Centertown, Illinois, to see Sarah. He pleaded with her to start over, to let him stage an intervention, to help her create a new and better life. He told her she could start over in Los Angeles, that she could be anyone she wanted to be, that she could shed her past like it was nothing more than a torn, dirty coat. But though she took the money he offered, she said she couldn't leave her friends or her boyfriend.

Every year he came back to try again to persuade her to leave, until a little over a year ago, when Sarah had told him that she knew how much he hated coming back to their hometown and that he didn't need to make the trip anymore. She'd sworn that his secrets were safe with her. She'd told him she was happy all his dreams had come true when he'd become Flynn Stewart. But she'd insisted she didn't have it in her to change herself and her life the way he had. She'd claimed they would both be better off apart, because then he would stop hoping fruitlessly for her to leave her life behind, and she would stop hating herself for disappointing him.

If only he'd guessed that she'd been hiding her pregnancy from him...

She must have known if he'd learned she was going to have a baby, he would never have taken no for an answer. He would have made her leave Centertown once and for all. He would have forced her to get the help she needed with her addictions. He would have shown her and her child that there was a world out there beyond her wildest dreams.

Flynn took the next flight out of LAX, careful once he landed to alter his look with dark-framed glasses, a baseball cap, and a worn pair of jeans and a faded T-shirt so that no one would recognize him.

It didn't matter how many years had passed, Centertown looked no different than it had when he was a kid. Despair lingered in the air, especially on the street corners where people were either looking for their next hit, or had already passed out from their last one.

Flynn stopped dead in his tracks when he looked through the window of the run-down, greasy diner and caught sight of Ruby sitting in a worn, dirty stroller.

She was the spitting image of his sister when she'd been a baby, with curly brown hair and big brown eyes. His chest clenched hard. Sarah was the only person Flynn had ever loved with his whole heart, holding nothing back.

Now, Ruby was the second.

As he slid into the booth across from Sarah's "friend," he knew from one look at her calculating, heavily made-up eyes made it clear that she wasn't simply going to hand Ruby over out of the goodness of her heart.

"Sarah said if anything ever happened to her, to call the name and number on this." It was a takeout menu from Pizza Peddler, the restaurant where Flynn and Sarah had had their last meal together. "She tried hard to stay clean while she was pregnant," the woman said with a shrug. He guessed Sarah wasn't the first person this woman knew who had overdosed. "Who are you anyway?" she asked. "You don't look like her usual type."

Flynn knew exactly what his sister's *usual type* was. A strung-out bully, just like their father. "I'm a friend from a while back," was all he said. Wanting to get Ruby away from her—and this place—as quickly as possible, he covertly slid over an envelope containing five thousand dollars in hundreds. "Thank you for calling me." Just thinking of what might have happened to Ruby if the woman had called anyone else made his stomach turn. Thank God she'd followed his sister's instructions.

Frankly, he would have paid any amount to get his niece the hell away from this woman, which was why he had plenty of backup bills ready to hand over if necessary. But five grand was more than enough to put skates on the woman's feet. She was gone so fast with his money, her seat at the diner practically smoked after she left.

Meanwhile, Ruby sat quietly in the dirty stroller and watched him with eyes that, thankfully, were still full of innocence.

He stared back, not knowing how to talk to a child, never mind a baby. Silently, he reminded himself that he wrote dialogue for fictional characters all day long. After all, Flynn Stewart was the first character he'd ever created, a guy with such a faultless, by-the-book, squeaky-clean past that no one had ever delved deeper to see if any of it was actually true. Surely he could figure out what to say to his niece.

"Hi, Ruby. I'm your Uncle Flynn," he said softly. "I'm going to take care of you now."

She stared at him for long enough that he half wondered if she could understand what was happening. Was there any way she could realize that she'd lost her mother forever and was now about to head halfway across the country with a total stranger?

Then the most miraculous thing happened—she smiled a big, gummy smile and reached for him.

Flynn's chest finally unclenched as he unbuckled her, lifted her out of the stroller, and pulled her close. "I'll never let anything bad happen to you," he promised her. "You'll always be safe with me. *Always.*"

The moment they returned to Los Angeles, he began the adoption process, pulling every string possible to get the paperwork through in record time. Though he had never planned to have kids—his family life had been so horrible that he couldn't imagine building a good, normal one himself—he already had to live with the guilt of knowing he hadn't done enough for his sister.

Whatever he had to change in his life for Ruby, he'd change. From this moment forward, Ruby and her stuffed toys and desire to be held every second of the day were the center of Flynn's world.

No more going out to splashy Hollywood parties to network with all the "right people." No more model girlfriend, either.

Anja had made it abundantly clear from the start that she wasn't the maternal type, which had been just fine with him back when he thought he'd never have children. When he'd told her Ruby was the daughter of a long-lost relative, Anja had been so uninterested in trying to make things work with him and a child that she hadn't asked questions. She'd simply packed up the things she kept in his loft for overnights, then left. And the truth was that once she had gone, what he mostly felt was relief at being off the hook for the endless string of parties and premieres she'd loved to attend.

Flynn had never been comfortable in the limelight, not when it meant people might look too closely at him and his past. After he'd been nominated for—and won—the Oscar for Best Original Screenplay, however, he'd inevitably ended up in the media more and more.

He could easily withstand stepping back from the spotlight. But he hadn't expected his writing mojo to up and leave too, as though he'd never been able to string together a coherent sentence before.

As he isolated himself with Ruby in those first weeks, the words drying up was far more brutal than losing his girlfriend or his social circle. All his adult life, he'd depended on making up stories to move him forward and keep him above water.

What would he do if that ability was gone forever?

Hoping the issue was simply that Ruby didn't sleep or eat on any kind of predictable schedule, which meant he didn't either, he hired a part-time nanny so that he would have a set time to write every day. The woman's qualifications looked good on paper, and though Ruby wasn't exactly a bundle of joy around her, at least if Flynn was within his niece's sight while he hunkered down over his computer and stared at the blinking cursor, she would tolerate the nanny changing and feeding her.

Every Monday through Friday mornings for two weeks, while the nanny tried and failed to coax a smile out of Ruby for three hours, Flynn tried and failed to coax a good scene out of his brain.

The day Smith's call came, Ruby had just gone down for a nap, and the nanny was sitting next to the crib reading something on her phone.

"How are you, Flynn?" Smith asked. "How's Ruby?"

Apart from Flynn's agent, his manager, and his ex, Smith Sullivan and his wife, Valentina, were the only other people Flynn had called after bringing Ruby home. Since Smith and Valentina were his bosses at present, waiting for him to send over his newest thriller script for their film and TV production company, he'd felt compelled to tell them at least the bare bones of the situation.

After giving them the same explanation he'd given Anja—that Ruby was the child of one of his long-lost relatives—he had insisted his changed family circumstances wouldn't affect the due date for his screenplay. Smith and Valentina had not only said it wouldn't be a problem if he needed a few additional weeks, they'd also been hugely helpful with getting Flynn set up with baby gear, sourced from Smith's large family.

Flynn waited to reply to Smith's question until he had moved into the back section of his house so that he wouldn't wake Ruby. "Ruby's good. And now that I've got a nanny to watch her for a few hours a day, I'm hoping to make some good progress on the screenplay."

"I'm not worried about the screenplay." But Smith *did* sound worried about something. "I'm calling because I just heard from a press contact that someone is trying to sell a story about you and Ruby to the media."

Flynn's heart stopped cold in his chest. He'd vowed to keep Ruby safe...and he was already screwing that up.

Could it be his sister's friend? Could she have figured out who he was after he'd left? Had the five grand not been enough for her? Or, could it be Anja? Although that didn't make much sense. She not only had plenty of money of her own, but she also wouldn't want to alienate him and his industry contacts by turning on him this way.

Then again, odds were Smith already knew the answer. Few people were more connected in the industry. "Do you know who's selling it?"

"It's your nanny, Flynn."

A split second later, he had dropped the phone and was running back to Ruby's crib, where the baby was still sleeping peacefully, thank God.

"Get the hell out of my house." He ground out the words to the nanny in a low voice, still intent on not waking Ruby, even though he was as furious as he'd ever been.

The woman's eyes were big as she looked at him. "Mr. Stewart, I don't know what you're—"

"I said *get the hell out.*"

Ruby's eyes opened then. All it took was one look at his face for her to start wailing. He picked her up, cradling her tightly against him.

"I won't tell anyone anything," the woman said in the short breaks between Ruby's cries. "Not if you don't want me to."

Flynn had been an idiot not to see the dollar signs in her eyes. "How much do you want?"

Her smile came slow. Satisfied. "Twenty grand."

Her satisfaction was short-lived, however. He picked up her bag, walked to the front door, and tossed it out on the street. He'd never had any intention of paying her a dime. He'd simply asked the question to confirm her mercenary intentions.

"You're going to regret this," she spat before slamming the door behind her, the harsh noise making Ruby cry even harder.

Flynn soothed her, rocking her, pressing kisses to her cheeks. Once she calmed down, he made her a bottle. She wasn't hungry, but chewed on the nib until she fell asleep again. Which was when Flynn finally remembered he'd left Smith hanging on the phone.

After gently laying Ruby down in her crib and covering her with a pink blanket, Flynn picked his cell phone up from the floor and found a text message waiting from Smith: *Don't worry, I've killed the story with every potential media outlet. Your nanny won't be able to sell it anywhere. Btw, my cousin has a cabin in the Maine woods. No one would bother you and Ruby there.*

* * *

*Present day…*

With one last, longing look at the bed, Flynn carried Ruby out to the open-plan kitchen and living room. She had been fussy all day—not that he could blame her. Two four-hour flights, plus a long and winding drive through the Maine woods in a musty-smelling rental car, weren't for the fainthearted. Add in a bunch of dirty diapers, bottles of formula that weren't exactly the right temperature, and a damned useless uncle, and you were in for a bumpy trip.

The cabin wasn't a dump, at least. Not that Flynn had thought it would be, given that Smith and Valentina had honeymooned here. But after having everything in his life go topsy-turvy, Flynn's expectations were low across the board.

It was the same lesson he'd learned over and over again as a little kid—knowing better than to expect anything good with two of the worst parents on the planet. It wasn't until he'd left Centertown for Hollywood, changed his name and backstory, then had a couple of hit screenplays under his belt, that things had begun to look up. In a big way, with gorgeous women throwing themselves at him and large sums of money landing in his bank account.

Ruby began to squirm in his arms, so he set her on the rug by a brightly colored stuffed elephant she seemed to want to play with. She wasn't yet crawling, but even if he hadn't already read every baby book on the market and learned that most babies crawled between six and ten months, he figured it was going to happen soon, simply because she was so intent on getting where she was going.

Though his bones felt like they were creaking from lack of sleep, he folded himself into a sitting position on the floor beside Ruby. If he walked away, she would cry. If he even sat on the couch five feet away, she would cry.

Again, he didn't blame her. Her life hadn't been easy so far. It was yet another thing they had in common—both of them had been born of adversity.

For Ruby, however, he vowed that she would climb out of it long before he had. No matter what he had to do to make it happen, she would know more triumph than failure, more joy than pain.

With Ruby happily playing with the stuffed elephant, he finally looked around their new temporary home. There was a vase of brightly colored wildflowers on the dining room table, a bowl of fresh fruit on the kitchen counter, and a cheerful mug with pens and pencils in it near the old-fashioned phone on the wall. The rugs were soft, the couches plush, and the kitchen table and chairs looked hand-built.

Flynn's place in Los Angeles was all sharp lines of glass and steel and polished concrete. This cabin, on the other hand, seemed to be made entirely of old wood and rock. Something stirred in Flynn, an innate feeling of comfort in this small cabin.

It wasn't something he'd thought he could ever feel

in a cabin in the woods. Not when he'd done everything he could to get away from the one in which he'd grown up. The bright, perpetual sunlight of LA, the endless pavement and concrete of downtown, the relentless heat—all of those things had saved him and would surely continue to do so once he got over this bump in the road. A few weeks away would surely be long enough for the dust to settle and for the media to move on.

At least, he hoped so.

He'd been rude to Smith's cousin Cassie. Not nearly as grateful as he should have been. Sorrow, guilt, and exhaustion were dark bedfellows. There was no question that he needed to apologize to her.

It wasn't just the riot of emotions he'd been dealing with for the past three weeks that had knocked him sideways when she'd opened the door. Cassie's face had lit up when she saw Ruby—and the glow that radiated from her had stunned Flynn speechless.

Cassie Sullivan wasn't built like a supermodel. She didn't have endless legs, hollow cheekbones, or cynical eyes that had seen it all.

She seemed the polar opposite, in fact. Her skin had been devoid of makeup. Her big eyes had been full of wonder, her mouth perpetually smiling. And she had curves too—lush curves that had stolen the words from his mouth and the thoughts from his head.

Damn it, Smith hadn't sent Flynn to this cabin in the Maine woods to hit on his cousin. To take her innocence and debauch her in every sinfully sexy way he could think of.

In any case, his days of thinking only of how to please himself were done. Ruby was the most important thing in his life from now on—not Flynn's instant attraction to a beautiful woman.

As though to drive the thought home, Ruby crawled onto his lap with a whimper, giving him a good whiff of her diaper. "Let's get you cleaned up and then see if you're in the mood to try some peas or carrots tonight."

Thus far, she'd wanted only a bottle. All day, however, she'd been gnawing on it more than drinking. Perhaps that meant she was ready for some solid food?

A few minutes later, though her diaper was clean and dry, she wasn't any happier. Not with creamed corn. Not with her bottle. Not with any of the baby toys in his bag, or the new ones Cassie had left in the cabin for her. Ruby even screamed in the bath, which she normally loved, her face getting redder and redder, her hands tightening into fists, her chest rising and falling with sad little gasps.

He tried everything he could think of. Walking with her, singing to her, even swaddling her, though she was clearly too big—and mad—to be happy wrapped up in a blanket. The sun set and the evening hours ticked by in a symphony of wailing and whimpering. And now, not just from Ruby.

Flynn was desperate for sleep. Far more than that, he was desperate for someone to help him help Ruby.

Was she sick? Had she picked up something on the trip? All he knew for sure was that he was screwing everything up…and that he couldn't do this alone.

He knew only one person in Maine. Smith's cousin Cassie. The woman he'd told, only hours before, that he wouldn't need anything else.

Served him right for being a grumpy jerk. He would grovel like no one had ever groveled before, if only Cassie could help him figure out how to make Ruby smile again.

Bouncing his miserable baby in one arm, he grabbed his phone with his free hand and dialed the number Cassie had left lying on the counter.

# CHAPTER THREE

*Four o'clock in the morning...*

Cassie rolled over in bed, hoping the ringing phone was just part of a bad dream.

She'd had a hard time falling asleep. Her insides had felt all jumbled up after meeting Flynn and Ruby. She couldn't forget the way they had clung to each other, like the only survivors of a shipwreck.

When the phone kept ringing, she finally accepted that she wasn't dreaming. She dragged on a robe over her pajamas, then headed into the kitchen, where she kept her phone charging at night.

The number wasn't one she recognized, but she knew the 213 area code from having shipped boxes of candy to customers in Los Angeles. Her heart seized with concern when she realized it must be Flynn.

"Flynn, is something wrong?" Why else would he be calling in the middle of the night?

"Ruby won't stop crying. She's been wailing for hours. Ever since you left." He sounded on the verge of tears himself. "I don't know what to do or who to call other than you."

"Does she have a fever? Or a rash?"

"No and no. She's barely been out of my arms for the past ten hours, and her temperature is normal. I've changed her and fed her and bathed her. She shouldn't have any reason to cry. But what the hell do I know?" The disgust in his voice at his own presumed incompetence was crystal clear.

"I'm sure you've done everything right, but I can come over now if you think that would help. I can be there in fifteen minutes."

"Hurry." Ruby wailing in the background was the last thing Cassie heard before the line went dead.

She didn't bother changing out of her flannel pajamas and robe, simply shoved her feet into a pair of mud boots by the door, grabbed her purse and keys, and ran out to her car.

Fifteen minutes had never seemed so long. Until she could see for herself that the baby was okay, she wouldn't be able to relax. Hopefully, Ruby was just tired and cranky from her long trip. If it seemed more serious than that, Cassie would call her mother for help. After raising seven children, Beth Sullivan was a bona fide baby whisperer.

Gravel spat from beneath Cassie's tires as she turned off the two-lane forest road to her cabin and raced up the long driveway. After throwing the car into Park, she ran up the brick path, able to hear Ruby's wails even from outside.

When Flynn opened the door, he looked nearly as red in the face as Ruby, whose cheeks were flushed dark pink and covered with tears.

"Oh, you poor baby." She nearly reached for the little girl again, but this time she knew to ask first. "Could I hold her for a moment?"

She thought he might say no. Until, with great reluctance, he let her take Ruby from him, the baby's body rigid as she kicked and screamed.

Cassie worked to stay calm as she assessed the situation. Ruby's diaper was new and dry, and her skin was surprisingly cool despite her crying. "Did you feed her anything new tonight?"

"She wouldn't eat. Wouldn't even drink her bottle."

"Has this happened before?"

"I've only been taking care of her for three weeks, but when she cries, there's always a reason. I thought maybe it was because of the flights and staying in a new place, but she's never cried for eight hours straight."

Ruby opened her mouth wide to let out another yell, and that was when Cassie saw it. A little flash of white in otherwise swollen gums.

"I think I might know what's wrong. She has a tooth poking through."

"Let me see." Flynn craned his neck to look into Ruby's mouth, which was right when Ruby decided to clamp it firmly shut.

"Has she been gnawing on things lately?" Cassie asked.

"Now that you mention it, I've had to replace the nib on her bottle twice today." He ran a hand over his face, looking ragged...but totally gorgeous nonetheless. "I've read every baby book out there, but my brain is so fried right now I'm blanking on what they said would help with teething."

"When my sister's son went through this, Ashley refrigerated twisted-up washcloths for him to chew on. She said it was a lifesaver." Cassie opened the fridge. "It would be nice if we could find something right now to give her immediate relief, though, so that we don't have to wait for some cloths to chill."

She was scanning the contents of the refrigerator when she noticed a pink and purple polka-dotted stuffed elephant sitting on the middle shelf.

When she lifted it out, Flynn groaned. "It's a good thing I'm not operating heavy machinery tonight. I had no idea I put that in there. It's one of the many things I've been trying to distract Ruby with tonight."

"Actually..." She held the toy to her cheek to test

its temperature. "This might be exactly what the doctor ordered." She brushed the stuffed toy lightly against the baby's cheek to get her attention, then mimed putting it between her own lips, before holding it up to Ruby's mouth. "This will make you feel a whole lot better, sweetie."

In a surprisingly fast motion, the baby grabbed the toy and shoved it into her mouth. Her big brown eyes widened for a moment at the unexpectedly cool temperature, but instead of spitting it out, she bit down.

It wasn't long before the rigid lines of Ruby's body began to loosen. Cassie felt her own limbs relax as she cuddled the little girl closer.

"Maybe, just maybe, we're out of the woods," Cassie whispered to Flynn, not wanting to startle the baby. "For now, at least."

He staggered into the living room and collapsed on the couch. *"Thank God."* His head was in his hands. "If something happened to Ruby... If she was sick and I didn't know how to help her... I would never forgive myself."

"Flynn." Cassie sat in the armchair near the couch, the baby cradled in her lap. "You've just come off a cross-country trip. You've done everything right, everything you could think of to soothe her. And then you called for backup. If I hadn't known what to do, I would have called my mom. If a mother of seven couldn't figure out what was wrong based on her experience, then we would have taken Ruby to a doctor, who would have found a way to make everything better." Without thinking, she put her hand over his. "Ruby is very lucky to have you."

His gaze slid from her face to her hand. She quickly pulled away.

Still chewing on the cool toy, Ruby rubbed her eyes. "You can go to sleep now, Ruby." Cassie smoothed her soft, dark hair, which was sticking up in damp tufts. "We'll make sure there are lots of cold things for you to chew on when you wake up."

When the baby lowered her head to Cassie's shoulder and closed her eyes on a deep, sleepy sigh of relief, Cassie's heart turned over inside her chest.

Love at first sight had already turned into something more. Something bigger.

That was when Cassie realized Ruby wasn't the only one falling asleep. Flynn's head rested against the back of the couch. His eyes were closed, the stress lines on his face smoothing out as he got the rest he so badly needed.

Her heart flipped again inside her chest. Only this time, it was for the totally out-of-reach man asleep on the couch in her cottage.

She didn't need the whole story of how he'd come

to be Ruby's guardian to know that he loved the little girl with all his heart—and that he would do anything for her.

Cassie was immeasurably glad that Smith had thought of her when they needed a place to stay. Hopefully, their time in the Maine woods would be something they would forever cherish.

Still holding Ruby, Cassie got up to stock the fridge with several other tiny stuffed toys and clean washcloths so that Flynn wouldn't be caught out again on the teething front. Ruby's tooth looked to be coming in quickly, so hopefully she wouldn't be in pain for too much longer. At least until the next tooth came in.

By the time Cassie finished setting everything up, Ruby was fast asleep on her shoulder, her grip on the polka dot elephant loosening enough that it dropped into Cassie's hand. She put the small stuffed animal back in the fridge, then sat carefully in the armchair so that she wouldn't wake the baby.

Putting large throw pillows on either side of them, she settled back to relax with Ruby in her lap until Flynn woke up. And though Cassie had a large to-do list to work through today—including making a start on a candy replica of Bar Harbor's Town Hall—her list paled against how glad she was to have been only a phone call away when Flynn and Ruby needed her.

★ ★ ★

Flynn woke up disoriented. *Where the hell was he?*

Then he saw Ruby sprawled across Cassie's chest, asleep, and it all came back to him.

His sister's death.

Finding out about Ruby.

The nanny's betrayal.

Flying to Maine.

Hours of Ruby crying.

And the miracle of finding Cassie—who was an out-and-out saint.

In Hollywood, people were rarely selfless. As far as he could tell, the Sullivans ranked among the few good ones.

Especially Cassie.

"You're awake." She spoke to him in a voice low enough that it wouldn't wake Ruby, a gentle smile on her lips. "I'm glad you were able to get some sleep." She looked down at Ruby, affection in her eyes. "Both of you."

He ran a hand through his hair, another over his eyes. "You saved me last night."

"I didn't do much. Just opened your fridge and found an elephant in it."

Her gaze was open and friendly as she smiled at him. In Cassie's eyes, he saw something rare. Something he hadn't ever seen before. No shadows, no lingering pain, no hidden sorrow.

If what he saw could be believed, Cassie Sullivan had never known how it felt to be truly hurt and disillusioned. It was exactly what he wanted for Ruby—for her to forget the difficult first six months and remember only joy as she moved through the rest of her life.

If he'd been more with it, he would have made sure Cassie knew precisely how grateful he was. That as far as he was concerned, she held the sun, the moon, and the stars in her hands.

"You should have woken me once Ruby fell asleep. You didn't need to stay." Even as the words came out of his mouth, he knew they were a far cry from the gushing praise he'd meant to give her.

"It was no problem." She lowered her cheek to the top of Ruby's head. "She's been lovely to sit with."

He would never have understood that sentiment before. But after three weeks with Ruby, he knew that having the trusting weight of a child in your arms was one of the best feelings in the world.

But since he'd never said something like that to anyone before, what came out instead was, "I'm sure you've got places to be now that the sun is up. I'll take her now."

As his words echoed back to him, he realized he'd

basically just told her to get out.

*Could he be getting this any more wrong?*

"I should have thought you'd want to hold her as soon as you woke up." She stood and carefully transferred the sleeping child to him.

It wasn't until she was pushing her feet into mud boots she must have kicked off at the door when she'd come in that he finally noticed what she was wearing. A thick pink robe over flannel pajamas that were printed with—

What was that animal on her leggings?

He could hardly believe it, even once he'd figured it out. She was wearing pajamas printed with two-toed sloths.

It was weird.

But also intriguing.

And, despite everything, sexy as hell.

The first time they'd met, she'd talked and talked until she'd let herself out the front door. This time, she merely gave him another small smile and then was gone before he had a chance to say thank you.

# CHAPTER FOUR

Cassie had to restart the candy base of the Town Hall building twice before she was happy enough with her work to continue. She was never at her best when she was tired, but though she hadn't had more than a handful of hours of sleep last night, that wasn't the reason for her constant stream of mistakes.

No, the issue was far more tightly tied to the gruff yet gorgeous man in her cabin—and his adorable baby. Just like the night before, she couldn't get them out of her head, or stop wondering how they were doing today.

Had Flynn managed to go back to sleep after Cassie left?

Had the chilled washcloths done the trick once Ruby woke up?

Had Ruby's tooth poked all the way through by now?

Cassie was on the verge of breaking down and calling Flynn for an update—one that would likely be monosyllabic, if their previous conversations were anything to go by—when Lola burst through the door, bringing with her the most wonderful gift imaginable. A coconut latte.

"I'll never admit to Ashley that I said this, but you're the best sister ever." Cassie grabbed the cup from her sister and gulped the sweet coffee down. Scalding the top layer of skin from her mouth and throat was worth it. Anything for a hit of caffeine when she so badly needed it.

"Long night?" Lola asked as she settled on one of the stools in Cassie's workroom. As always, she lifted cake stand covers one after the other to see if there was anything that caught her fancy. At last, she settled on a red velvet cupcake.

"Short night, actually. I didn't get much sleep."

The doorbell rang before Lola could ask why—a double ring that meant Doug was here with a delivery. As Cassie's hands tended to be covered in sugar, she'd asked him to let himself in so that she didn't have to stop work and wash her hands before opening the door.

"Good morning, Cassie." His eyes lit up when he saw she wasn't alone. "Lola, you're looking exceptionally lovely today."

Lola smiled around a mouthful of cupcake. "Hi, Doug."

As kids, even before Lola's figure could have made

Marilyn Monroe jealous, Cassie's sister had had a knock-out effect on boys. By the time she was eighteen, it seemed like every man in Maine was begging to go out with her. Doug was just as smitten as the rest. Amazingly, however, the endless male adoration hadn't gone to Lola's head.

Several beats later, Doug remembered the box he was holding. "Sorry to interrupt your work, Cassie, but you've got to sign for this one."

She washed her hands, signed to acknowledge receipt, then gestured toward the cake trays. "If you're hungry, I've got lots for you to choose from."

She didn't need to offer twice, and though he seemed sad about leaving Lola behind, he was soon on his way out to continue his deliveries, a cupcake in each hand.

"I wonder what this could be?" Cassie gave the box a light shake. "I wasn't expecting anything."

"That is the exact color of Tiffany jewelry boxes." As a textile designer, Lola knew color inside out. More than once, Cassie had asked for her help with mixing the right hue for one of her candy creations.

"Well, I certainly haven't ordered anything for myself from Tiffany. And I can't think of anyone who would want to buy me expensive jewelry. In fact, I can barely remember the last time I was on a date."

"*Men.*" Lola scowled.

Cassie didn't envy Lola's looks. With va-va-voom curves that made people do a double take and her fifties-style fashion sense that further highlighted her hourglass figure, people often mistakenly thought she was flighty and dumb. Nothing could be further from the truth—Lola was absolutely brilliant, and happiest when she was quietly creating. Unfortunately, the men who asked her out tended to be interested only in her bombshell exterior.

"I can't believe I almost forgot to tell you that Brooke sent over a new box of chocolate perfection." Cassie opened the small fridge beneath her worktop and took out the prized dark chocolate truffles her cousin Rafe's wife made in the Pacific Northwest. Though Cassie worked with chocolate from time to time, candy confections were where her real talent lay. "Who needs men when we've got these?"

Lola put the last half of her cupcake down in favor of popping a truffle into her mouth. *"Ohmygoshthisisamazing."* She was too gaga over the chocolate to separate her gushing words. "I love Brooke. Rafe's such a lucky guy."

"I agree." Cassie let a truffle melt slowly on her tongue, too busy savoring the delicious treat to pay much attention to what was beneath the egg-paper wrapping of the small box she found inside the larger cardboard box Doug had just delivered.

"Cassie." Lola went from gushing to dead serious in a heartbeat. "That's *definitely* a Tiffany box."

Pulling off the rest of the wrapping paper to reveal an elegant, oblong velvet case, Cassie realized her sister was right. "There must be a mistake. I can't think of *anyone* who would send me something from this store."

"Open it already," Lola urged, "so we can find out what it is and who it's from."

Cassie popped open the case...and they both gasped.

*"Oh my God."* Lola slid off her stool to get a better view. "Look at all those diamonds. And there's a note. Quick, read it!"

Cassie slid a tiny card out of a small blue envelope.

*Thank you for everything. You're a lifesaver.*

*Flynn*

Lola's gaze flew to Cassie's face. "Flynn?"

"He's Smith's friend who needed a place to stay," Cassie reminded her sister. No one in her family had assumed Flynn was anyone famous, and it hadn't occurred to her to tell them he was a famous screenwriter. Especially not when she knew he'd wanted to come to Maine to get away from his fame. "He arrived last night."

"Did Smith also happen to mention that his friend is the kind of guy who says thank you with diamonds?" Lola took the bracelet out of the case and held it up to the light. "This is absolutely stunning."

It was. But that was irrelevant. "I can't keep it."

Lola looked mildly horrified at the thought of Cassie giving it back. "Why not?"

"Because it's way too big a thank-you for helping him out last night."

"Wait. I thought you were just letting him stay in your cabin for a little while. What else did you *help him out* with last night?"

Cassie rolled her eyes at her sister's dirty mind as she took the bracelet and laid it carefully in the case. "With his baby, Ruby." Cassie's heart softened the way it always did when she thought of the little girl. "You should see her, Lola. She's *beautiful*."

"Wait… You're not talking about Flynn Stewart, are you?"

"That's him."

*"Oh my God."*

"You're starting to sound like a broken record."

"That's because only you would forget to tell me that *Flynn Stewart* is the guy we've been talking about this whole time. What's he like?"

"Honestly, I don't really know. We've barely spent any time together." All she knew for sure was that he would do anything for Ruby. And that he wasn't a fan of Cassie sticking around the cabin, unless absolutely necessary.

"You were obviously together for long enough that he felt compelled to send you diamonds."

"I don't want to gossip about him, especially when I'm guessing that's part of the reason he needed to get away from Hollywood." Cassie frowned. "How did you guess so easily it was him?"

"I heard that an actress was wearing a dress made of one of my fabrics. While I was on the website, I read a rumor that Flynn had become the guardian of a baby a few weeks ago, then left town in a rush. There's all kinds of speculation about whose baby it really is." She held up her hands, looking a little guilty. "I know I shouldn't read that stuff, but I swear I'm not asking you to gossip about him. All I'm asking is if he's as hot in person as he looks in the press?"

Cassie couldn't keep the heat from flooding her face at the memory of exactly how *hot* Flynn truly was.

Lola grinned. "That's a yes. In all capital letters *and* bold font."

Cassie looked down at the diamond bracelet. "I can't believe he thought he needed to send me a gift like this when all I did was help him settle Ruby down." She was pretty sure it wasn't gossiping to tell her sister, "The baby was teething and wouldn't stop crying, and my number was the only one he had in the area."

"What time did all this take place?"

"Four."

*"In the morning?"* Lola was doubly horrified. "Sorry, but not even Flynn Stewart is good-looking enough to warrant getting out of bed that early."

"I'm glad he called." Cassie knew she sounded defensive, but after the night she'd shared with Ruby and Flynn, she felt extremely protective of both of them. "Ruby was miserable, but once we figured out that she was teething and gave her something cold to chew on, she settled down. I already told him I was happy to help, so he should have known that there was no need to send me this." She popped the jewelry case shut. "Honestly, who gives someone a diamond bracelet for helping with their baby for a few hours?"

"By this standard," Lola agreed, "Ashley owes us *piles* of jewelry." Their nephew, Kevin, was ten years old and an extremely independent and self-sufficient kid. When he'd been a baby, however, all of them had pitched in to help Ashley out when they could, so that she could finish high school and then get her business management certificate at the nearby junior college.

"I've got to return this bracelet to him immediately." Cassie gestured to her progress—or lack thereof—on the Town Hall commission. "I'm useless here today anyway."

At least now she had an excuse to check on them.

"I'd ask you to tell him that you have a sister you want to set him up with," Lola said, "but you're right—helping him with a baby definitely doesn't warrant a gift like this. I have a feeling he's got a crush on you."

"A crush?" Cassie felt herself blush so hard, her face might have just gone purple. "That's impossible."

"Why? You're gorgeous, smart, talented, successful."

"That's nice of you to say, but I'm pretty sure he only dates supermodels."

"Guys like him always think they want a supermodel, when really what they're craving is homemade apple pie. You're full of so much sweet and wholesome goodness that any guy with half a clue would want to take a bite out of you."

Cassie couldn't help but laugh as she locked up her studio behind them. "You have been watching *way* too many episodes of *The Great British Bake Off*."

"Bite your tongue," Lola scolded. "There could *never* be too many episodes of British people baking in tents on big estates."

Laughing at the paradox of her sister, who had never sifted flour or used a mixer, being far more passionate about TV baking shows than anyone she knew, Cassie gave her a hug, then headed over to her cabin to return Flynn's over-the-top gift.

# CHAPTER FIVE

Mid-morning, when the doorbell rang, Flynn immediately tensed up at the thought that the paparazzi had already tracked him down. He'd been careful not to leave any clues as to where he was going, and he knew Smith wouldn't have told anyone. Maybe someone Flynn had encountered during his cross-country travels with Ruby yesterday had seen through his glasses-and-hat disguise?

All of which made it a distinct pleasure to find Cassie standing on the porch.

Ruby had just woken up from a short nap, but as soon as she saw Cassie, she held out her arms.

"Hello, gorgeous." Cassie pressed a kiss to Ruby's forehead as she took the baby from him and cuddled her. They walked inside. "You look like you're feeling a million times better."

As if to agree, Ruby pulled the chilled stuffed elephant out of her mouth and thrust it in Cassie's face.

Laughing, Cassie took it, made it walk through the air, then put on a silly voice to say, *"My name is Ellie the elephant, and I love polka dots and little girls named Ruby."*

Ruby clapped her hands, her gummy smile even wider now.

Flynn had been struck by Cassie's looks from the first—her sexy curves, luminous skin, and open, friendly smile already set her apart. But when she was making Ruby laugh, she truly was the most beautiful woman he'd ever set eyes on. Kindness radiated from her like a beacon of hope.

It was exactly the kind of sweet, caring hope that Flynn and his sister had never known when they were growing up. And exactly what he hoped Ruby would know from this moment forward. Somehow, some way, he needed to figure out how he could give that to her.

"You're good with her," he said. "Really good." He wished he had even a tenth of her natural know-how and comfort with babies. But until Ruby had come into his life, he hadn't been around a baby since his sister was born. And he'd been only a toddler himself at that point.

"So are you," Cassie said, obviously just being kind. She rubbed her cheek against the top of Ruby's head. "I can't tell you how relieved I am to see that she's feeling so much better."

"You and me both." Flynn winced as he thought back to the hours of crying the night before. He'd felt so hopeless, terrified that he was doing absolutely everything wrong for Ruby. "I can't thank you enough for racing over here in the middle of the night to help."

"That's actually why I'm here—to give back your thank-you gift."

"Why?"

Before replying, she made Ellie the elephant dance in the air some more, humming a little tune in the funny voice. Ruby was giggling at her antics when Cassie said, "I already told you that I was happy to help out last night. You didn't need to give me anything. Especially not a diamond bracelet."

In his experience, women loved diamonds, no matter the occasion. But the look on Cassie's face as she took the Tiffany box from her bag and placed it on the kitchen counter made it perfectly clear that he had overstepped his bounds. Big-time.

Wanting to make it up to her, he said, "What *can* I do for you, then?"

"If you're really this adamant about showing your gratitude, I suppose you could take me to lunch."

"Great. How does lunch right now sound?" As if to second the motion, Ruby made a happy sound—a *loud* happy sound. "As long as you know somewhere baby-friendly, that is. Our restaurant outings on the road to get here didn't go all that well."

Cassie grinned. "I know exactly the place."

★ ★ ★

"This is my family's restaurant." Cassie pointed to the Sullivan Café awning above the front door and the outdoor seating area. "It's the best Irish country food on the East Coast. On any coast, if you ask me."

Cassie and her siblings had grown up underfoot in the downtown Bar Harbor café. As far back as she could remember, her mother had brought each of them into the kitchen. First, to play. And then, when they were older, to help.

Of the seven of them, Cassie was the only one who fell in love with being in a kitchen. By the time she'd graduated from high school, Cassie knew how to make all of the Irish specialties, from beef and Guinness stew to Dublin coddle. But it was making desserts that most captured her interest. She'd graduated from the Culinary Institute of America in New York, then came straight back to Bar Harbor to open Cassie's Confections. But Cassie wasn't the only of her siblings whose future had been shaped in some way by the family café and Irish gift boutique. All of them had, in one way or another.

Lola had loved to decorate the café and source pretty items for the store, so it was no wonder she went on to design textiles.

Rory had helped build the tables, chairs, and shelving for the café. He was a highly sought-after bespoke furniture designer now, but he still made pieces for the family business in his spare time.

Turner had drawn the most remarkable pictures of Ireland to hang on the walls. No one had been at all surprised when his illustration skills took him into the animated-film business.

Brandon had been instrumental in convincing their parents to expand the business beyond Bar Harbor and into other parts of Maine. Though he was frequently on a plane to exotic locales to open new hotels, he kept a close eye on the health of the family business.

Long before Hudson had earned his degree as an architect, he had drawn up plans for their new locations in Camden, Portland, and Kennebunkport.

And even as a teenager, Ashley had enjoyed wading through receipts and making—and taking care of—to-do lists. She was the perfect person to head up the day-to-day management of the Sullivan Café "empire." Plus, her hours were flexible enough that she didn't need to put Kevin in after-school care.

Cassie, Flynn, and Ruby had barely set foot inside the café when Cassie's mother, Beth, came out to greet them. She always seemed to know when a baby was on the premises.

Cassie quickly made the introductions, impressed that her mother waited until she was done to ask,

"Could I hold Ruby, Flynn?"

Though he hesitated, just as he had with Cassie the first time she asked, he ended up agreeing. Of course, Beth had Ruby giggling within seconds. Flynn seemed both surprised and impressed with how well Ruby had taken to a complete stranger.

"Your little girl is absolutely beautiful," Cassie's mother said. "And obviously extremely smart too. Her eyes are so bright—she's interested in everything around her."

"Yes," he agreed, "she's pretty darn special." He reached out to stroke Ruby's cheek before turning back to Beth. "Cassie says you own this café. There are few things I enjoy more than good Irish country cooking."

"Then you're in for a treat," Beth said with a twinkle in her eye, her Irish accent strong even after more than three decades in America. "Would you like me to puree some fruit or vegetables for Ruby's lunch?"

"She hasn't taken much interest in solids yet," Flynn replied. "I'd hate for you to go to any trouble."

"It's no trouble at all. How about I make up a couple of things to see if we can tempt her? In fact, if you don't mind me taking her into the back, my kitchen staff are all just as crazy about babies as I am."

Flynn didn't answer right away, clearly torn over whether he could stand to let Ruby out of his sight. However, when Beth made her giggle again, this time by tickling her tummy, he nodded. "As long as she's happy, I'm okay with it."

"Don't worry. If she starts to fuss, I'll bring her right back to you. Why don't you let me warm up a bottle for her too, just in case?" Flynn handed over Ruby's baby bag, which he'd loaded up with diapers and formula and extra clothes before they left the cabin.

"We're going to take that table in the corner, Mom." Though Flynn hadn't said anything about remaining anonymous, when he'd slipped on his hat and glasses after getting out of the car, it had been a clear cue that he didn't want anyone to recognize him.

"Great," Beth said. "Here is the list of specials. Amy will come take your order in just a minute."

Flynn looked a little dazed as they sat down, and not from lack of sleep this time. "Your mom is very nice. And a bit of a whirlwind."

Cassie smiled. *Whirlwind* was the perfect description of her mother. No wonder he was an award-winning screenwriter—he obviously had a way with words. "She's pretty darn special."

When he realized she'd echoed his comment about Ruby, he smiled back. And wow…did it ever do crazy things to her insides. It felt like a dozen butterflies were now flying around inside her stomach.

Hoping to cover her reaction to him, she said, "My

mom is a baby whisperer. I swear even babies on the street see her and stop crying."

"You're a baby whisperer too, you know." He smiled again, making even more butterflies go wild. "We wouldn't have made it through last night without you."

Suddenly, it occurred to her that this was the first time the two of them had been alone. Okay, so there were other people eating in the café, and Amy had come over to gape at Flynn with the menus still clutched in her hands. But as soon as Cassie took the menus so that Amy could drool over him from across the room instead, they were effectively alone again.

And she was fighting a losing battle against getting lost in his deep-blue eyes.

"You would have been just fine without me last night," she insisted. "It was blind luck that I happened to see the tooth poking through her gum. It probably also helped that I wasn't jet-lagged."

"It's not jet lag that's the problem." He ran his hand over his chin. "You're probably wondering what the heck is going on. Why I've been taking care of Ruby for only three weeks and where her mother is. I don't know what Smith told you, or what you've read—"

"You don't need to explain anything to me, Flynn."

He scanned her face, as though he was trying to see all the way into her heart. Finally, he gave a little nod, like she'd just passed some invisible test. "You've been so generous. You shouldn't have to be completely in the dark. Plus, I don't want you to believe whatever you might see in the press." He paused briefly before telling her, "My sister passed away recently."

Her heart broke for Ruby and Flynn all over again. "I'm so sorry."

"I am too." Sorrow was etched into the lines of his face. "It was never public knowledge that I had a sister—still isn't." The words were clearly a warning, one she wanted to tell him he didn't need to give her. She would *never* gossip about him to anyone, not even her family. "I wasn't able to see much of her over the years. Not nearly as much as I would have liked. But as soon as I found out she died, I had legal custody of Ruby within forty-eight hours."

"What about your parents? Are they able to help at all?"

"They're also dead." It wasn't sorrow that passed over his face this time, but an emotion that looked a whole lot closer to anger. His gaze flickered away from hers. "Car crash."

"Oh, Flynn." She reached out to put a hand over his for a brief moment—long enough to register how warm, and strong, he was. "You've both been through so many changes in such a short time. I wish there was something more I could do to help, other than just offering my cabin and a few teething tips."

"You've helped more than you know. Life in Hollywood…" He shook his head. "It isn't where Ruby needs to be."

"What about you? I'm assuming most of your business meetings take place in Los Angeles."

"They do, but when I'm deep in a new script, I deliberately avoid them. Nothing ruins creativity faster than listening to some guy in a suit drone on about audience segments and profit margins."

"I deliberately avoid meetings too," she agreed. "Unfortunately, my lack of business acumen is currently reflected in *my* profit margins."

As she was speaking, he shot another glance toward the kitchen. He'd been doing that since they'd sat down.

"I'm sure Ruby is doing great in the back with everyone," Cassie said softly, "but if you'd feel more comfortable having her out here with us, Mom would be happy to bring her back to you."

She could see how much he wanted to have Ruby close by. Badly enough that he seemed to be fighting a silent battle with himself before saying, "Ruby looked like she was having fun with your mom. It's good to see her laugh." He turned his focus back to Cassie. "You made her laugh too. Thank you for that."

Cassie felt her cheeks go hot under the intensity of

his gaze. "Anytime."

Beside the table, Amy cleared her throat. How long had she been standing there? Long enough to see Cassie turn beet red just because Flynn was looking at her?

"Do you two know what you'd like to order?" Amy asked.

"I'd like the colcannon fish pie," Cassie said, "and a coconut latte."

"I'll have the Irish stew," Flynn said, "with an espresso."

"So," Cassie said once Amy walked away. She had to have at least one conversation with Flynn where she didn't get so flustered. "You were saying you're deep into a new screenplay."

"Smith and Valentina are waiting on a new thriller. Only, I'm not sure when I'm going to be able to work on it now that I have more than just myself to think about."

"I'm sure you want to spend as much time as you can with Ruby—who wouldn't? But have you thought about bringing in a nanny for a few hours every day?"

His expression darkened. "I tried that back in LA. Suffice it to say that it didn't go well."

"Did the nanny hurt Ruby?" Fury rose inside Cassie.

"No, thank God. But she did try to sell our story to

the media."

"That's horrible." Cassie couldn't understand how people could be so mercenary. "Some of my well-known cousins, like Smith, have had issues like that in the past. I always feel so bad that they have to go through it."

"It's the price an adult who has chosen a career in the spotlight pays for notoriety. But kids should *never* be put in a position like that."

"I totally agree." As soon as her mom brought Ruby out, Cassie wanted to give the sweet little girl a hug.

"Smith is the one who intercepted the story," Flynn told her. "I owe him big-time."

"You didn't buy him a diamond bracelet, did you?"

She wasn't sure if she'd been right to tease Flynn, especially during such a heavy conversation. But she hated seeing him look so upset.

Thankfully, the corner of his mouth quirked up. "Nope. He looks better in emeralds."

As Amy dropped off their drinks, Cassie laughed, glad that he no longer seemed quite as tense.

"You've been so much help so far," he said. "You don't happen to do a sideline in thrillers, do you?"

"Not only can I not write worth a darn, I'm also too much of a scaredy-cat to watch anything dark or twisty."

"Surely you've seen a thriller before."

She shook her head. "My cousin Lori loves to say that I'm all butterflies and rainbows. Which is actually right on point when it comes to the kinds of movies I like to watch."

"What's one of your favorite movies?" he asked.

She nearly laughed out loud at the movie that immediately popped into her head. One she had a feeling Flynn would never have watched in a million years. "*Trolls.*"

"*Trolls?*" He leaned forward as if to interrogate her. "Are you talking about the animated film where they sang all those songs from the eighties?"

"It was very heartfelt."

He blinked at her as if he couldn't believe what she'd just said. "Heartfelt." He seemed to roll the word around inside his mouth.

"I even have the soundtrack on my phone." Instead of being embarrassed, she was having fun throwing him for a loop. "Cyndi Lauper's 'True Colors' has never sounded better."

Finally, he laughed. And if his smile had made a few butterflies go wild in her stomach, his laughter was like having dozens of them shooting around inside of her.

"After all the years I've spent in the movie business," he said, "I should know by now that we've all got different tastes."

"What got you into thrillers? Were they always your favorite?"

"Actually, the original version of *The Adventures of Robin Hood* is at the top of my list."

"My dad is a big fan of that Errol Flynn movie too." She was happy not to sound like a complete greenhorn. "How perfect that you share the same name as the star of your favorite movie."

Something passed across his face, an expression she couldn't quite read. It was gone by the time Amy had finished delivering their food.

"What about you?" he asked. "What do you do?"

"I make candy."

"Like Willy Wonka?"

She laughed. "Kind of. Only, I don't shrink any kids or blow them up into giant blueberries."

"That's a relief." He took a bite of his Irish stew, and the look on his face said it all. "This meal is one of the best I've had anywhere."

Cassie beamed. "Say that again when Mom comes out of the kitchen, would you?"

As if she'd conjured them up, Beth walked back into the dining room just then, carrying Ruby. The baby was wearing a green and white baby bib embroidered with four-leaf clovers and the words *I'm so cute, I must be Irish.*

Amy brought over a high chair, and after giving it

good wipe down, Beth slid Ruby into it. "Sean will bring over some apple puree for Ruby to try in a moment. She looked very interested in it when he was preparing it."

"This is delicious, Mrs. Sullivan," Flynn said, gesturing to his plate. "Truly the best Irish food I've eaten."

"Call me Beth. And thank you." Cassie's mom beamed at Flynn. "You and Ruby are welcome to eat here anytime. In fact, if you're free Friday night, why don't you come to dinner with Cassie and the rest of the family? My grandson, Kevin, loves playing with other children, and I'm sure Ruby would have a wonderful time with everyone. Plus, I want to make sure I see her again soon."

Cassie almost groaned at her mom's hard sell. Especially because she couldn't help but suspect she had ulterior motives. Beth Sullivan had always been a matchmaker. The fact that it hadn't worked yet didn't deter her in the least.

Though Flynn looked surprised by the invitation, when he saw the way Ruby was grinning up at Beth, he readily agreed. "Dinner on Friday night sounds great. Thanks."

Sean carried over a green plastic bowl shaped like a four-leaf clover that he'd filled with apple puree and set it on Ruby's tray. Beth pressed a kiss to the baby's cheek. "Enjoy your meal, my little treasure. I'll see you on Friday."

Flynn handed the spoon to Ruby, then gently placed his hand over hers, dipped the spoon into the apple puree, and brought it to her mouth. She sniffed it, then shoved it into her mouth. Most of the sauce landed on her bib, but what did make it onto her tongue obviously pleased her, as she immediately tried to scoop up more.

Cassie grinned. "I think she likes it."

Flynn was also grinning as he helped the baby with her second bite. Again, most of the applesauce went onto Ruby's bib—and hands and hair and legs—but she didn't seem to mind at all. On the contrary, she seemed absolutely delighted.

Fifteen minutes later, Ruby wasn't the only one covered in applesauce. Both Cassie and Flynn had been splattered with more than their fair share.

Flynn gently wiped Ruby's face and hands. "You need a bath," he said in a soft voice to her. Then he looked down at himself and Cassie. "We all do."

Ruby replied by rubbing her eyes with the backs of her sticky hands. She reached out to Flynn, who lifted her from the high chair and settled her against his chest, making Cassie's heart melt again. They were the sweetest pair.

"Sorry to eat and nap, but I think I'd better get this

one off to bed. I think she's still making up for last night." He smiled at Cassie. "Thanks for lunch."

"It was fun." Especially once she'd been able to act like a normal human being, rather than a blushing fool. Maybe Flynn's effect on her was wearing off.

She almost snorted at that thought. It was so ridiculous, considering every one of his smiles lit her up inside like a Fourth of July celebration.

"Are you sure I can't convince you to keep the bracelet?" he asked.

"Nope, you can't."

"Well, then we'll see you Friday for dinner."

"My workshop is only a couple of blocks from my parents' house. If you come by around five thirty, we can walk over together." She stroked Ruby's back. "Have a good nap, cutie."

Flynn and Ruby had only just left the café when Cassie's mom sidled up to her. "Ruby is lovely. So is Flynn."

"Thank you for being so wonderful to both of them," Cassie said, "but don't even think about matchmaking."

"Me? Matchmake?" Her mother adopted her most innocent expression. "I wouldn't dream of it."

"Seriously. You know how I feel about being set up. It's always a recipe for disaster. Smith needed a favor for his friend and colleague. Any one of us would have stepped up to help. End of story."

"So you don't find Flynn attractive?"

"*Mom!*"

Beth put an arm around Cassie, not the least bit repentant. "Ruby reminded me of how lovely it is to hold a baby. It's been a long time since Kevin was that small. You can't blame me for wishing for more grandchildren, can you?"

Cassie decided it was wisest not to reply. "Thanks for a great lunch. I've got to get back to work now. See you Friday."

On her short walk back to her workshop, the air seemed sweeter, the sky a brighter blue, the town square prettier. Cassie wasn't naïve enough to think it was coincidence.

No, she understood exactly what had happened to her: Despite knowing just how far out of her league Flynn was, and despite her protests to her mother, she had not only fallen head over heels for Ruby, she had also fallen for the baby's handsome, brilliant, over-whelmed uncle.

Cassie's mother hadn't needed to do any match-making at all.

# CHAPTER SIX

Flynn always avoided places that reminded him of where he'd grown up. He worked out in a gym, rather than outside surrounded by trees. He vacationed in big-city skyscrapers, never in a log cabin. And he deliberately chose to live in one of the busiest, most-pavement-heavy cities in the world. Had he not felt trapped by the media vultures in Los Angeles, he would never have come willingly to the Maine woods.

And yet, after three days, Flynn was surprised by how much he enjoyed the smell of the fallen leaves mulching on the ground, the smog-free blue sky, the honest physical effort of chopping wood to make a fire, and especially the quiet. As for Ruby, she was never happier than while strapped to his back in a baby carrier as they hiked through the trees, her eyes huge with wonder as he pointed out squirrels and birds and flowers.

For the first time, it occurred to him that he didn't actually hate nature and its lush green forests. No, what he hated was the way he'd been raised, with shame and anger and not an ounce of the love that Cassie's mother, Beth, showed her own children. Ruby, too, who had lapped up both her affection and her apple puree.

His gut twisted every time he thought about the half-truths he'd told Cassie in the café. She was the first person he'd told about his sister, the only one who knew that Ruby was his niece. But he'd immediately followed that up with a lie about his parents dying in a car crash.

Lying had never sat right with Flynn, but at seventeen it had seemed like the only way he could start fresh without being dragged down by his family history of drugs, booze, and misery. He'd not only changed the story of his life, he'd changed his name, too, renaming himself after the actor who starred in his favorite movie, a tale in which the hero fought back against his oppressors—and won. Once he started telling those made-up stories to his new friends and colleagues in Los Angeles, he was soon in too deep to climb out and come clean.

All the while, he justified his behavior by telling himself that he hadn't hurt anyone by shedding his past and becoming someone new. What's more, he would have given anything to bring his sister out West so that she could start over too. If only she had agreed before it was too late…

Cassie was different, though. She wasn't hard or jaded or fake like so many of the people he knew in Hollywood. She was a nice person doing a nice thing for him and Ruby.

Which was why lying to her made Flynn feel like the lowest of the low.

For the first time since he was seventeen, he found himself thinking seriously about coming clean. Only, it wasn't just his future at stake anymore—it was Ruby's life, Ruby's future, that mattered most.

Again and again over the past three days, he asked himself the same questions: What was the best thing he could do for Ruby? Keep pretending that there were no shadows in their past? Or admit it all, regardless of the consequences, and forge a new path forward?

His gut continued to churn as he checked Ruby's diaper bag to make sure they had everything they might need for their evening out. Less than a month ago, he would have been mixing cocktails in his high-tech kitchen for Anja and her friends before heading out to a hot new restaurant in Beverly Hills. As he gave Ruby a last-minute change, due to a leaking diaper, the contrast couldn't have been bigger. She happily kicked her legs as he stripped off her dress, wiped her down with baby wipes, then put her in new leggings and a top with yellow and green butterflies.

*Butterflies and rainbows.* That was how Cassie had

described her movie-viewing choices. Last night, he'd found *Trolls* on a streaming service and put it on for Ruby to watch, thinking she might enjoy the bright colors and singing. She had fallen asleep in his lap not long after the opening credits. Flynn had continued watching, however, and had been surprised by how much he'd enjoyed it.

*Heartfelt* was right on the money. And the story wasn't half bad either. After nearly two decades spent writing movies, Flynn could spot a story hole or character-motivation misstep from a mile away. He couldn't think of much he would have done to improve the screenplay. What's more, he couldn't deny that the characters—cheerful Poppy and grumpy Branch—reminded Flynn of the two of them. Cassie, at the very least, seemed like she might break out in song at any moment.

No one in Hollywood would dare admit to preferring a movie like *Trolls* over the latest dark and brooding Oscar contender. The more esoteric and artsy a film was, the more people in the business fawned over it. Even when the truth was that they were bored out of their minds while watching it.

Once he was done changing Ruby, Flynn lifted her up and hugged her to him. Who would have guessed that big one-toothed smiles and clean baby skin beat cocktails and models any day of the week?

Twenty minutes later, he and Ruby were knocking on the door to Cassie's Confections.

"Hi." She opened the door with powdered sugar dusted across her cheek. "I just need to set the thermostat for the evening so that nothing melts." She reached for Ruby, and the baby happily went to her. "Aren't you a sight for sore eyes?"

She nuzzled the baby's cheek as she took them past a room with a desk and filing cabinets, then down a short hallway. He'd expected a candy store, but this looked more like the entrance to a commercial kitchen.

"How have the two of you been doing the past few days?" she asked.

"Good. I was inspired by your mom to make Ruby some puree—" His mouth fell open before he could finish his sentence. "You said you made candy."

"I do. All of this—" She gestured to the large work in progress on the wide stainless-steel countertop, which looked like the foundation for a building. "—is candy."

"This isn't just candy." He scanned photos on her walls of what he assumed were other structures she'd made. "You create *masterpieces*." That was when he realized something else. "I've seen your work before. Smith has used your confections in a couple of his movies, hasn't he?" He circled the worktable. "You have the most incredible eye for detail. How do you do it?"

She looked a little shell-shocked by his praise. "You know what a good cook my mom is. It was easy to learn from her. And speaking of my mom, we'd better get going before all the bacon-and-cabbage rolls are gone. My siblings eat like savages. I'm warning you, if you don't want to walk away hungry tonight, be bold and pushy when you're filling your plate." She tapped a few buttons on the thermostat by the door, then gestured for them to head out.

But he wasn't ready to stop admiring her work. She was so talented that his jaded Hollywood mind was blown. "Is there anything you've made that I can taste before we go?"

"Sure." She took a tray out of one of her many stainless-steel refrigerators. "This is a sushi-style candy. It's a really popular style in Japan." It really did look like a sushi roll. "It's sweet, but with a little kick at the end."

The sugar melted instantly on his tongue, followed by a hit of spice and heat.

Cassie not only had a gorgeous face and a kind heart, she was a brilliant confectioner as well.

"That was extraordinary."

*She* was extraordinary.

Her skin flushed pink at his compliment. "Thank you."

"Honestly, I think it might be the best thing I've ever put in my mouth."

And as Cassie flushed an even deeper rose, he couldn't help wondering if *she* would also taste as sweet...

★ ★ ★

Flynn was more nervous than he wanted to admit about tonight's dinner with the Sullivans. He hadn't spent much time around families during the past twenty years, not when life with his own had soured him on the idea of *family*.

Beth greeted them at the front door. "Flynn, Ruby, Cassie—I'm so happy you're all here!" Just as she had at the café when the three of them walked in, Cassie's mother took Ruby into her arms. "I've missed you so much, my little treasure."

In response, Ruby reached out happily to pat Beth's cheeks, making them both laugh.

Settling the baby on her hip, she said, "Come on in and meet everyone, Flynn, while I get you both a drink."

"We can take care of our own drinks, Mom." Cassie turned to Flynn. "What's your poison?"

Three fingers of whiskey would go a long way toward taking the edge off. But Smith hadn't connected Flynn with his aunt, uncle, and cousins so that he could get drunk in their house. He also hadn't suggested Flynn stay in Cassie's cabin so that he could seduce her...

"A beer would be great. Thanks."

As though she could tell he was nervous, Cassie said, "My family can be a bit much to take in if you're not used to a million people all talking at once. There are seven of us, not including my parents, but two of my brothers aren't in town tonight, so that will save you trying to remember a couple of names."

Seven siblings. He couldn't wrap his head around it. Flynn had been close to his sister when they were young, and it had felt like the two of them against the world. But once she'd hit her teen years, there had been nothing he could do to keep her out of harm's way.

The next thing he knew, he was in the middle of a group of men and women who had all stopped talking to stare at him.

"Everyone, this is Flynn, and the adorable little girl in Mom's arms is Ruby."

Flynn had been worried that Ruby would be overwhelmed by so many new people and yet another new house. Fortunately, she seemed fascinated by everything around her—the food, the people, the house, and especially the enormous fluffball of a dog lying on the floor in front of the stove. Clearly, that was the place to be if you wanted to catch falling food.

"Flynn, meet Rory, Turner, Lola, and Ashley." Cassie scanned the kitchen for someone else, finally finding him in the view from the window. "There's Kevin, Ashley's son, in the backyard. He's ten." She squatted down to scratch between the dog's ears. "And this is Bear."

Flynn shook hands with Cassie's brothers and sisters. The family resemblance was strong—the Sullivans had all been cut from very attractive cloth—but at the same time, they were each distinct. Rory was rugged looking, and judging by the calluses on his hands, he obviously worked with them. Turner, though as broad in the shoulders as his brother, was not nearly as tanned, nor were his shoes as scuffed, so Flynn guessed he worked at a desk. Ashley had delicate features and seemed to be the quietest of the bunch. She barely looked old enough to have a ten-year-old son. Clearly, there was a story there. And then there was Lola, who looked like she'd walked straight out of a fifties pinup calendar.

He knew plenty of guys who would fall hard for both Ashley and Lola. But though they were beautiful women, Flynn didn't feel the slightest hint of a spark with either of them. Not the way he had from the first moment he'd set eyes on Cassie.

"And this," Cassie said as a distinguished-looking

man walked into the room, "is my dad, Ethan. Dad, this is Flynn, Smith's friend who is staying in my cabin. And this is his little girl, Ruby, who I'm sure Mom hasn't stopped talking about since we saw her at the café earlier this week."

Ethan Sullivan's grip was strong, his voice deep…and his eyes held a definite warning. *Don't mess with my girl.* "It's good to meet you, Flynn. I'm glad you and Ruby could join us for dinner tonight." *So that I can keep a close eye on you.*

Flynn had never met the fathers of any of the women he'd dated. Not that he and Cassie were dating—she was a million times too good for the likes of him. Which her father had clearly sussed out at a glance.

"Thank you for having me to your home."

Every eye remained trained on him, and though he'd had to prove himself a hundred times over in Hollywood, tonight felt more difficult than any of those film-studio meetings.

He wasn't here to prove that he was talented. Instead, he was trying to live up to being given a seat at the Sullivan family table. To make matters worse, he had no idea what any of them knew about him. Not when the bits of press that he'd seen during the past three weeks served only to stoke the mystery of who Ruby's mother might be—and what else he might be hiding in his past.

Cassie handed him a beer and one of the coveted bacon-and-cabbage rolls.

Turner broke the ice. "I'm a big fan of your work. I've watched *Silent City* many times."

"You wrote that?" Ashley looked pleasantly surprised when he nodded. "You're really talented."

"Thanks." Though he appreciated the praise for his work, Flynn was never comfortable in the spotlight. He'd much rather turn the focus on someone else. That way, there was a smaller chance of screwing up and getting a piece of his story wrong.

Cassie seemed to sense his discomfort, because she said, "Turner works in movies too."

Flynn had thought her brother looked familiar. "You're Turner Sullivan, the animator."

Before Turner could reply, Cassie told him, "He worked on *Trolls!*"

Everyone laughed at her enthusiasm, with Lola informing him, "It's one of her favorite movies, if you were wondering."

"I know." Flynn was glad to feel much more relaxed now that he was no longer the absolute center of attention. "I watched it last night."

"You did?" Cassie clearly couldn't believe it. "What did you think?"

"The story was good." He smiled at her before adding, "Heartfelt." He turned back to Turner. "And the animation is great."

"Thanks. I'm always happy when I can work on something my nephew and my cousins' kids can watch."

"What are you working on now?"

"A Japanese anime series." Flynn recognized the name Turner gave him, though he hadn't read the books the series was based on. "What about you?"

"I'm sitting on a partial screenplay. Although I haven't been able to do much with it in the past few weeks." Again, he wasn't sure how much Cassie's family knew, but he couldn't live with himself if he didn't at least tell them the same truth he'd already admitted to her. Hoping that none of them would spread the news any further than this house, he said, "My sister passed away three weeks ago. Ruby is her daughter." His chest clenched as he looked across the kitchen at the little girl who meant everything to him. "She's mine now."

Everyone told him how sorry they were about his sister, then Beth called from the stove, where she and Ruby were stirring something in a big pot, "If you need help babysitting, I'm more than happy to help."

"That's very generous of you, but I couldn't ask you to do that."

"Are you kidding?" Cassie said. "I haven't seen

Mom look this happy since Kevin was a baby."

"Truly," Beth agreed as she stepped away from the stove to lower Ruby to the floor to meet the dog, "it would be my pleasure to spend a few hours a day with this little cutie while you're staying in town."

All of them, all of this, was so nice. Too nice. Flynn was afraid to trust it. Afraid to let himself enjoy it. Afraid that just when he let his defenses down, it would all disappear as though it had been nothing more than a mirage.

Lola, who didn't seem at all shy, elbowed him in the ribs when he didn't reply quickly enough for her liking. "Say yes, or you'll break her heart."

Flynn desperately needed the hours with his screenplay. What's more, every day for the past three weeks, he and Ruby had been attached at the hip. Literally, she sat on his hip most hours, her arms around his neck.

The last thing he wanted to do was let Ruby leave his side when he couldn't shake the fear that something might happen to her while he was gone. But courtesy of the countless baby books he'd read while Ruby slept in his arms, he also knew this wasn't a healthy pattern to set. He needed to create some independence and boundaries for both of them before they created an unbreakable, and untenable, routine.

In the end, however, what swayed him was seeing

how happy Ruby was in the Sullivan family home as she patted the dog's fur.

Beth said, "Doggy."

Ruby made a happy sound, one that was nowhere close to *doggy* but filled his heart all the same.

"In that case," he said, "I'll take you up on your generous offer."

Cassie's mother's grin lit up the room. "Did you hear that, Ruby? The two of us are going to have so much fun!" She clapped her hands, and the baby mimicked her. "I set up a portable crib and baby monitor in one of the bedrooms for tonight so that you can tuck Ruby in when she gets tired, instead of trying to keep her up until the end of dinner. And I've made some more apple puree if you think she's hungry now."

"I'm sure she is. Although you didn't have to do that." He pulled several covered bowls out of the baby bag and placed them on the kitchen island next to the high chair they had put out for Ruby. "She liked what you made at your café so much that I experimented with making a few purees for her too."

He put Ruby in the high chair, wiped her hands clean of dog hair with baby wipes from his bag, and tied a bib around her neck. Though she wasn't thrilled about being taken away from her new furry best friend, as soon as she realized it was dinnertime, her eyes lit up.

Grabbing her purple plastic spoon, she dove into her food as soon as he pulled the top off the plastic container. Soon, pureed vegetables were flying onto her face, clothes, and hair.

Ashley laughed. "Kevin was just like that when he was a baby. His food went everywhere but in his mouth. But boy, did he have a great time eating."

"What was I like?"

Flynn turned to see Ashley's son standing at the kitchen door that led to the lush, well-landscaped backyard.

Ashley smiled at her son. "Kevin, this is Cassie's friend Flynn and his little girl, Ruby."

Flynn went over to shake the boy's hand. "Hi there. It's nice to meet you."

"Hey." Kevin's grip was surprisingly strong. "It's nice to meet you too."

Flynn remembered being that age, halfway between a kid and a teenager. His body had felt like it was growing too fast and in weird ways. Girls were suddenly interesting, but he hadn't been sure why.

Ten was also when he'd finally been unable to ignore how different his family was from everyone else's. They weren't really one, for starters. And the other kids at school all turned on him, saying his parents were dirty and smelly and drunks and losers.

"I was just saying how much you liked playing with your food when you were Ruby's age."

At last, Ruby noticed Kevin. Her eyes grew big. As far as Flynn knew, she'd never played with another kid before. She couldn't take her eyes off Ashley's son.

"I could help you feed her if you want." Kevin tried to say it like he didn't care either way, but it was obvious he was just as curious about Ruby as she was about him.

"Sure," Flynn said. "I'll bet she'd love that."

"Wash your hands first." Ashley shuttled him over to the sink, where he did the world's fastest soap-up-and-rinse. "And be careful with her. She's really tiny."

"She's not *that* tiny." He walked over to her high chair. "Hi, Ruby." He spoke to her as though she were a peer, rather than nearly ten years younger. "I'm Kevin." Ruby's one-toothed grin was her own brand of introduction. "What do you want to eat next?" He squinted at the bowls. "How about this green stuff?"

"Peas," Flynn supplied.

Kevin made a face—*ewww, peas*—but he fed it to her anyway. When that bowl was empty, he moved on to the apple puree Beth slid in front of them.

That was when it hit Flynn that he didn't need to stand guard over Ruby in Cassie's parents' house.

It was the strangest feeling.

For the past three weeks, since he'd paid off his sister's friend so that he could bring Ruby home with him, every breath he took, every move he made, had been with Ruby's safety and happiness at the forefront. Heck, until Beth had taken Ruby into the kitchen at the café, he hadn't let her out of his sight.

An unexpected wave of relief moved through him. Not because he was glad to be free from watching over Ruby for a little while. It wasn't that at all.

No, it was relief at having unexpectedly found a group of truly good people. And knowing instinctively that they wouldn't hurt his little girl—unlike people in Hollywood, who were only after the biggest paycheck they could get selling their stories. Granted, Smith and Valentina were two of the best people he'd met in Los Angeles, but he'd always felt that they were an anomaly.

From a writer's perspective, Flynn couldn't help but be intrigued. How had they built such a loving family? What were their motivations and goals? What life experiences had made each of them who they were? Especially Cassie's parents.

"Everything is ready to be brought to the table," Beth announced. "Flynn, why don't you move Ruby to the high chair in the dining room?"

After transferring Ruby, he sat on one side of her, while Kevin claimed the other side. She seemed to be full, so he put a few plastic toys on the tray for her to rattle and chew on. By the time he looked up from rooting around in her baby bag, a feast had been laid out on the large dining room table.

"This all looks delicious, Beth." His mother had barely been able to boil water without setting the house on fire. Honestly, until tonight, he hadn't realized family meals like this even existed outside of movies and TV shows, where he'd assumed they must be figments of the writer's imagination. "When did you learn to cook so well?"

"My grandmother was the best cook on the west coast of Ireland. I grew up in the kitchen helping her with whatever she would let me get my hands into. When it came time to have a career of my own, cooking was all I wanted to do."

Cassie smiled as she told him, "My parents met in Ireland when my dad ate at my mom's restaurant for the first time."

"It wasn't *my* restaurant," Beth clarified. "Have you heard of Ashford Castle?"

"I spent a few nights at Ashford Castle when I was doing some research for a movie. It's a very impressive hotel." And the location couldn't be beat—on the Mayo-Galway border on the shore of Lough Corrib. "You were chef at the George V?"

Beth laughed, shaking her head. "I was at the *very* bottom of the totem pole, barely a step up from dishwasher, which I also did when they needed someone to fill in."

"Dad—" Cassie turned to her father. "Tell Flynn how you reacted when you tasted Mom's food for the first time."

Her father held Flynn's gaze for a beat longer than was comfortable. Though Ruby had come through with flying colors, Flynn knew *he* was still on shaky ground. Especially with Cassie's brother Rory and her father, who had eyed him in silence since he'd walked in the front door.

Finally, Ethan spoke. "I had never tasted anything so good in all my life. Leek and potato soup with warm soda bread." He licked his lips just thinking of it. "I had to meet the person who made it."

Flynn flashed back to the Japanese-inspired candy Cassie had given him to taste earlier that evening. He had already been intrigued by her—but after tasting the breathtakingly good candy that she'd made with her own talented hands, he was downright fascinated.

"He nearly got me fired." Beth pretended to scowl at her husband, but it was clear that her words were full of love. "You see, he hadn't ordered off the extensive menu. Instead, he'd told his waitress that he was sick of fancy five-star restaurant food and wanted to eat good, simple country cooking that an Irish family would eat in their own home. Since the chef was in a meeting with the manager of the hotel, my friend who took his order goaded me into making my grandmother's specialty."

Ethan reached for her hand, staring into her eyes. "It was absolute perfection. To this day, I've never been able to adequately describe just how happy your food made me."

"And I've never been able to adequately describe the look on the chef's face when he realized he hadn't made the meal you were going on and on about." Beth made a face as she explained to Flynn, "Chef was furious when he came back to the kitchen to find out who had made the *abomination*. All these years later and I'm still quaking in my shoes at the memory of it."

But Ethan was shaking his head as though to disagree with her on that point. "I didn't notice any part of you quaking when you finally agreed to come out so that I could lavish on you the praise you deserved. Only that you were the most beautiful woman I had ever seen."

"You weren't too bad yourself," she said with a grin. "But you still had a tan line on your ring finger." Beth turned back to Flynn as she added, "A good Irish girl made sure to notice things like that, especially when she worked at an international hotel full of men who were more than happy to hide their wedding rings during business trips."

"I was newly divorced and had just sold my company," Ethan explained. "Traveling around Ireland exploring my roots was my way of working out what I wanted to do with the rest of my life." He put his hand over Beth's. "You weren't the least bit impressed with me, were you?"

"You already knew how impressive you were, given that everywhere you went, women fell at your feet. It seemed far safer simply to be your friend."

Cassie's father sighed. "It took me two months to convince Beth to date me, and six more before she agreed to marry me and move to America. She not only showed me the Ireland of her heart during those months, she also fed me her favorite dishes, one after the other. By the time we left, I knew I wanted to share my newfound love for Ireland—the food, the people, and especially this beautiful woman sitting beside me— with the world."

"Thank you for telling me your story." Even if Flynn had sat down with a list of questions for Cassie's parents, he doubted he'd have been given such insight into them. As he always did, he stored away the information to utilize for possible characters in his screenplays.

Now that he had told his own story, Ethan turned his hawklike gaze on Flynn and asked, "What brings you to Maine?"

"I thought it would do Ruby and me some good to get out of Los Angeles."

"Why is that, exactly?"

That was the question he'd hoped no one would ask. It figured Cassie's super-protective father would aim straight for it with an arrow.

Before he could reply, Cassie knocked over her glass, spilling water onto both of their plates.

"Oops! Flynn, can you help me clean up?" She was already standing and had both of their plates in hand. "You guys keep eating."

She looked upset as she scraped their soggy food into the garbage. "I'm sorry for that. My dad knows better than to stick his nose into your business. And he wasn't even subtle about it!"

"Don't be sorry." Flynn was surprised to realize how much he hated seeing Cassie upset. "I'm having a good time. So is Ruby."

"Are you sure? Because we can leave if—"

"Cassie." He tugged on her hands to get her to stop apologizing, inadvertently pulling her closer. "Everything's okay. You don't have to fight my battles for me."

"You shouldn't have to fight them alone."

No one had ever said something like that to him before. "Cassie—"

Lola burst through the kitchen doorway, causing

Cassie to pull her hands from his and jump back as though they'd been caught doing something illicit.

"You guys okay in here? Because Papa Bear is starting to get restless with the two of you out of his sight."

Cassie shot Flynn an embarrassed look. But he got it: Ethan Sullivan would do anything to protect his children, just as Flynn would go to the ends of the earth to keep Ruby from harm.

★ ★ ★

Thankfully, the rest of dinner passed without incident.

Ruby slept in the portable crib in a back bedroom for most of dessert, with Kevin staying near to make sure she didn't wake up frightened at being alone.

Flynn had seemed to enjoy discussing great filmmakers with Turner. He was also surprisingly knowledgeable about couture fashion houses, due to research he'd done for a screenplay early on in his career, which meant that he and Lola got on like a house on fire. He'd even managed to get Ashley to talk about her job managing the family business, which was an impressive feat, given that she tended to be quieter than the rest of them. And then, he'd offered to wash the dishes, which had endeared him even further to her mother.

Only Rory and Dad had been holdouts. Cassie had always respected her dad and brother, confident that they only ever acted out of love for her. But she couldn't see what they hoped to gain by behaving like this tonight.

They were clearing the table when a wail sounded from the baby monitor. A beat later, Kevin came running out. "Ruby's upset!"

Cassie could see the fear on Flynn's face as he raced into the bedroom, Kevin on his heels. She wanted to go with him, wanted to reassure him that whatever Ruby needed, he would be able to give her.

Before she could, Kevin ran back out with an update.

"Her diaper was full." He scrunched up his face. *"Really* full of *poo."*

Ashley laughed. "In that case, let's give Ruby and Flynn some space to take care of the situation. You can help clear the table."

A few minutes later, Flynn walked out with Ruby in his arms. She was rubbing her eyes and looked like she might start crying again at any moment. "Beth, would you mind if I took a rain check on the dishes? I think it's time to get Ruby home to bed."

Warmth spread in Cassie's chest that he'd called her cabin *home.*

"Of course." Beth gave Ruby a kiss and both of them a hug. "Thank you for joining us tonight. We're all so glad you came." Cassie couldn't help but think that her mother had deliberately used the word *all* to try to overcome her husband's obvious reticence. "And don't forget, I'm planning to start babysitting tomorrow. How does nine to noon sound for our first day?"

"It sounds great. And you're a marvelous cook, Beth. Thank you for the best dinner I ever had." He looked around at Cassie's siblings and her father. "Ruby and I appreciate the warm welcome to Bar Harbor." Then he shook hands with her brothers, father, and Kevin—whose chest puffed up with pride at being counted among the men—and hugged her sisters.

As Cassie walked Flynn and Ruby to his car, which he'd left by her office, he said, "You've got a great family."

"I know. Although I'm sorry that my dad and Rory were acting a little weird. I honestly don't know what their problem is tonight."

"I do." Just then, Ruby leaned forward to put her arms around Cassie's neck for a cheek nuzzle, and Flynn moved closer too. "You're a beautiful, kind, talented woman, and they want to protect you from anyone they think isn't good enough for you."

Stunned, she felt her mouth drop open. "But they've got to know you couldn't possibly be interested in me!"

He was standing near enough for her to see the

golden flecks in his blue eyes as he said, "A man would have to be a fool not to be interested."

She couldn't breathe quite right as he stepped away to buckle Ruby into her car seat.

Then he said, "Good night, Cassie," and drove away.

* * *

By the time Cassie got back to the house, her parents were relaxing with a glass of port on the backyard patio, while her siblings washed pots and dishes in the kitchen. Taking her place in the cleaning assembly line, she picked up a towel to dry the plates that had been washed.

"Your date doesn't like talking about himself much." Rory had a cynical glint in his eyes as he scrubbed a frying pan. "Almost like he's got something to hide."

"He wasn't my date," Cassie protested. But no one seemed to hear her.

"You're not being fair, Rory." Ashley put away a wine glass in an upper cabinet. "We all know how hard life can be in the public eye." There were no superstar actors or singers in their immediate family, but there were several of each among their cousins and their spouses. "Besides, I thought he was great with Ruby." It was a *massive* compliment from Ashley, given what a tool Kevin's father was. Being a great parent was at the very top of her list of positive male attributes. "He seems like a natural father, which is especially impressive given that he's only had custody of Ruby for three weeks."

Rory handed the pan to Turner to rinse, then began scrubbing the bottom of another. "What do you know about Cassie's guy, Turner?"

"He's not my guy!" Cassie said. But again, it was as though they had aimed the mute button at her. Her lips were moving, but none of them were listening to a word.

"You know I keep my nose out of the Hollywood gossip columns as much as possible," Turner replied. "The only thing I know for sure is that his work is good."

"We all know that," Rory said. "But I'm not talking about the fact that his latest thriller was a mind-bending triumph. You must have heard something about his personal life. Does he party? Is he a spotlight hound? Is he all about fame and fortune? Or is he just in Hollywood because that's where the work is?"

"Like I said, I don't know the guy very well. We've been at a few of the same industry events, but we never met until tonight, and I don't remember him dancing on the tables, or anything like that. Just that he had a different woman on his arm each time."

Rory scowled. "I knew something was up with that guy the minute I saw him."

*"Enough!"* Cassie gripped her kitchen towel so tightly that the seams started to separate. "He's staying in my cabin, not marrying into the family. So what does it matter how he chooses to live his life?"

"Are you honestly trying to say you didn't notice how his eyes followed you all night?" Rory asked. "Every word you said, every move you made, he didn't miss a thing."

No matter what Flynn had just said to her on the sidewalk, she still found it impossible to believe he could be interested in her. "You do know who he's been dating, right?" Cassie said to Rory. "I'm sure you can find your copy of the latest swimsuit issue of *Sports Illustrated* if you need a reminder."

Rory turned from the sink. "Don't underestimate yourself, Cassie. So what if he was dating a model? He clearly isn't looking for one now."

Even though she'd just insisted Flynn wasn't interested in her, she had to nail her brother with, "Thanks for the compliment."

"You know what I mean. You're not a bikini model, but you still look perfectly fine."

"Again," she said with a shake of her head, "you really know how to boost a girl's confidence."

He threw up his soapy hands in defeat. "All I'm saying is, I want to know more about the guy since he's clearly interested in you."

"And all *I'm* saying is that he's come to Maine to spend time with Ruby out of the spotlight, not to find a new girlfriend." Cassie loved Rory. She was also more than a little concerned about the fact that he hadn't quite seemed like himself this year. But that didn't mean she was going to let him walk all over her. "You and Dad embarrassed me tonight by acting like you need to protect me from him. What's more, even if he *is* interested in me, I don't need any of the men in my family puffing up their chests and beating them in a show of dominance. Because I'm more than capable of looking out for myself."

Lola and Ashley both clapped at the end of her soliloquy, while Rory and Turner wisely kept their mouths shut as they finished doing the dishes.

# CHAPTER SEVEN

Silence had never been so *silent* before.

The following day, after Flynn dropped Ruby off with Beth, he had headed with his laptop to the library.

The red brick building just off the Village Green in the center of Bar Harbor was impressive, both inside and out. Libraries had always been Flynn's secret getaway spots. In Los Angeles, where people loved to work in cafés with headphones on, he far preferred working at the public library. Fortunately, the Los Angeles Central Library was so enormous he could always find a quiet corner to himself.

At last, he was able to dig into his screenplay today with no interruptions. He should have been elated to get back to his normal life, if only for a few hours.

But he already missed Ruby so darn much.

She had been happy as a clam about spending time with Beth, giggling the moment they'd walked through the front door. Flynn, on the other hand, had hung around the house far longer than he needed to, worried that Ruby might start crying or fussing when she realized he was going to leave. He might never have left at all if Beth hadn't given him a hug, told him everything was going to be just fine, then pretty much pushed him out the door.

At the polished wood table, instead of focusing on the draft of his screenplay, he checked his phone again, in case Beth was trying to reach him. Of course there were no messages. After raising seven children, there was likely nothing she couldn't handle when it came to babies.

Okay then. It was time to get to work. He had only two and a half hours left until he picked up Ruby, so he'd better make the most of them.

Unfortunately, within ten minutes of reading through his partial script, he was dismayed to realize that the words on the page rang false—almost as though he was reading someone else's work.

Maybe because...in many ways, the past three weeks *had* turned him into someone else?

Before Ruby had come into his life, he hadn't had to care about anyone but himself. Sure, he had friends and women he dated, but each of them was best at looking out for themselves, scrapping for whatever piece of the pie they could get.

He'd been as bad as any of them. Worse, even, because he'd built his current life out of lies about his past. He'd told himself it was everything he wanted—a glittering, celebrity-filled life that he could never even have dreamed about as a kid growing up in abject poverty in the middle of nowhere.

Now, however, when he looked at his Los Angeles life, it seemed so lonely. So pointless. So much like a treadmill that never actually went anywhere.

Life with Ruby certainly wasn't easy. And he still wasn't sure he had the faintest clue what he was doing.

But at least he was making a difference in someone's life.

Looking at his screenplay again, he knew without a doubt that there was nothing he could do to fix it. He'd been a selfish bastard when he'd written these fifty pages, and that was that.

Flynn clicked on the file and dragged it into the trash.

He was behind schedule, but he'd still harbored hope that he'd get the screenplay in on time. He'd never missed a deadline before, but he'd definitely have to ask Smith and Valentina for an extension.

*What the hell was he going to write about now?*

Flynn's brain had always meandered in dark and suspenseful directions. When he was a little kid, even on the nights when his father hadn't been actively giving him nightmares, his overactive imagination had sent him spiraling down dark, deep holes. As an adult, it had been easy to turn those childhood nightmares into twisted scenes of emotional and physical devastation for his screenplays.

But now, for the first time in his life, Flynn didn't want to spend the bulk of his time peering into dark corners and imagining the worst. He couldn't get something Turner had said at dinner out of his head: *I'm always happy when I can work on something my nephew and cousins' kids can watch.*

Flynn hated the thought of Ruby seeing one of the terrifying, violent movies he'd written. Surely she'd know that only someone with half a heart could have made up stories like that.

But how could he write anything else when he hadn't ever known true happiness himself, or a loving family dynamic like the Sullivans had?

Last night, Cassie's family had laughed so easily together. They'd teased one another. They'd looked after one another. And Cassie's father and brother were clearly hell-bent on protecting her from any man who didn't pass muster. Which Flynn definitely didn't.

Considering how much of his life he'd spent telling lies, he should have been better at continuing to lie to himself. But when it came to Cassie, there wasn't any point.

Yes, he was fascinated by Cassie's family.

But he was far more fascinated by *her*.

No woman had ever been further out of his league.

He was well suited to actresses and models, women who knew how to put on a mask and wear it profitably. After all, that was exactly what Flynn had been doing his whole life.

Cassie, on the other hand, was as honest as a person could be.

Her smile was real.

Her beauty wasn't painted on.

Her laughter came from her heart.

Even her business was wholesome and sweet.

He'd never considered writing a character like her, because he'd never known anyone like her. And as he sat in the silent Bar Harbor library and stared up at the vaulted wooden ceiling, he couldn't deny that he desperately wanted to learn what made Cassie tick.

He wanted other things too. Things that involved stripping off her clothes and hearing her gasp with pleasure. Not just once, but again and again, until her voice was hoarse and her skin was flushed from his lovemaking.

Flynn knew better, though. Her father, her brother—they were both right about him. Just because he wanted her didn't mean that he was anywhere near good enough for her, or even close to being the fairy-tale prince that she deserved.

No, he could never have her as his own.

But would it be so wrong to ask her to help him

understand the joy, the light, the hope that she felt, so that he could find a way to put all of those things in a screenplay and, much more important, share them with Ruby as he raised her?

A flicker of excitement ran through him at the thought of basing a character on Cassie.

Particularly the part where it meant spending plenty of time with her to get things right.

He closed his laptop, slid it into his leather bag, then headed out of the library. If Cassie was game to help him one more time—even though he already owed her more than he could ever repay—the next time he came back to the library to write, he hoped to have a whole lot better idea of the story he wanted to tell.

Her candy-filled office was only a handful of blocks away. Though Flynn had assumed he'd feel claustrophobic living in a small town again, after nearly two decades of needing to drive everywhere—if you could call sitting in bumper-to-bumper traffic with thousands of other bitter commuters *driving*—he found he enjoyed being able to walk from Cassie's parents' house, to the library, to her office, in only three tree-filled blocks.

He knocked on the door, then rang the bell when there was no answer.

Had she headed off to lunch with another guy? His

gut clenched as he thought about her laughing over Irish food with some jerk trying to woo her into his bed. Flynn had a feeling she had to bat away men like flies.

Or was she simply elbow-deep in caramel or powdered sugar and couldn't answer the door without washing off first? Working to push away the *very* evocative visions that created, he decided to try the knob.

No one would dream of leaving their door unlocked in downtown Los Angeles. In Bar Harbor, however, it seemed perfectly normal. Yet another difference between this small town and the one he'd grown up in, where no one was safe, even when their doors were locked.

"Cassie?" He called her name as he walked through the small entryway, then down the hall to her workshop. "It's Flynn."

"Flynn?"

He could hear panic in her voice and then what sounded like two voices hissing at each other.

"Wait," she called. "Don't come back—"

But it was too late, because he was already halfway through the door to the workroom. And for the second time, his mouth dropped open.

# CHAPTER EIGHT

At the sound of Flynn's voice, Cassie jumped away from Lola so quickly that half a dozen pins pricked her.

Her sister had been measuring and draping muslin for the past half hour. Pieces of the thin fabric were pinned over Cassie's body, so she wasn't exactly naked. Unfortunately, though Lola planned to sew a liner for the dress next, at this point they were still working on the nearly see-through material that would make up the pattern for the dress—and with the sun shining through the window from behind Cassie, she had a feeling the fabric was likely transparent.

What was doubly unfortunate was that the bra and panty set Cassie wore was pretty much see-through too.

"What are you doing here, Flynn?" Her voice was both breathy and squeaky.

"What my sister means," Lola said, her voice laden with humor, "is hello, it's nice to see you again."

Cassie had made the mistake of doing one too many Google searches last night, so she knew that

Flynn hadn't dated just one model. He'd dated several. Worse still, the word *super* was usually printed in front of the word. Which explained why he hadn't stopped staring at her since he'd walked in.

This was probably the first time he'd ever seen a normal female body.

At last, he dragged his gaze away from her mostly naked skin and smiled at her sister. "It's nice to see you too, Lola." Too soon, he turned his focus back to Cassie. His eyes were dark and unreadable as he said, "I figured your hands must be sticky, so you couldn't answer the door."

"No." The word came out a squeak. "I haven't started work yet."

Though she was practically flushing neon with mortification, he still didn't turn to leave. Instead, he said, "I haven't started working yet either. I need to talk with you first."

Couldn't he see that she was *dying* of embarrassment here? "Maybe after Lola and I are done, we can figure out a time to talk."

"Actually," Lola cut in, "I have everything I need, so you guys can talk now."

In one deft move, her sister pulled a few pins from the muslin and whipped the fabric from Cassie's body. Which left her standing in only her bra and panties and the heels she'd put on so that her sister could accurate-

o his arms. But Flynn looked like a man on a mis-
n—and not one that involved hearts and flowers
her.

"Why did you need to talk with me?"

"I was reading through the draft of my screenplay
the library when I realized it was all wrong. I trashed

She looked up from her worktable. "Oh no." She
ew how hard it could be to get partway through a
ject before facing up to the fact that it wasn't going
work. "Again, I'd offer to help, but my brain has
ver worked in a twisty-turny sort of way."

"Actually, I think you're *exactly* the person who can
p."

He'd surprised the heck out of her when he'd
lked in on her in her underwear. But hearing that he
ught she could help him with his screenplay was
nost more of a surprise.

"How do you possibly think *I* could help?"

"I'm going to start the script from scratch. New
ry. New characters. And I'm playing with basing one
the characters on you."

Any secret hope that she'd had about Flynn having
romantic interest in her died in that moment. Last
ght, when he'd said how any guy would be a fool not
be interested in her—sweetly seductive words that
d played inside her head, over and over again, ever

ly assess the length of the dress. Thankfully, at this
point, Flynn turned his back like a gentleman.

"I'll have something for you to try on in a couple of
days, Cass. I hope to see you and Ruby again soon,
Flynn." In a flash, Lola was gone.

Cassie scrambled for her clothes, tripping over her
heels. The first thing she could easily reach—a thin
white apron—was next to useless without jeans or a T-
shirt to wear beneath it. She nearly cried out loud with
relief when she wrapped her fingers around denim.

She'd never been the most elegant woman in the
world, but she hadn't been this uncoordinated either.
First, her toes got stuck in the leg of her jeans, and then
she tried to stick her head through an arm of her shirt.

By the time she was fully dressed again, she was a
flustered, sweaty mess. Her hair must be a halo of frizz
around her head. And she was panting as though she'd
just sprinted around the block.

After shoving her hair into a messy ponytail and
taking a few deep breaths, she finally found her voice.
"You can turn back around now." After he did, she
said, "What was it you needed to talk about? Ruby isn't
having trouble at my mom's, is she?"

"I texted to ask if everything was okay five minutes
after leaving your mother's house, and she sent me a
picture of Ruby laughing. I figure that's her way of
saying I should stop worrying. It's not easy, though. I

know spending some time apart from me is good for Ruby, but..." He ran a hand through his hair. "I can't stop worrying that something bad will happen to her if I'm not watching over her every second."

Cassie couldn't help but fall just a little bit more for him when she saw such love in his eyes as he talked about Ruby. "I'm sure everyone feels the same way the first time they leave their little one with a babysitter."

Clearly uncomfortable with the conversation, he bent to pick up a pin from the floor. "Does your sister make a lot of your clothes?"

"Only for special occasions."

"What's the special occasion?"

"I'm up for an award." When he looked impressed, she held up a hand. "It's nothing big, like the Oscars or Emmys that you must be used to. Once a year, there's a nationwide contest for best new confectioner, and I lucked out and made the finals, which happen to be just down the coast in Portland next weekend."

"I very much doubt luck had anything to do with it. You don't give yourself nearly enough credit, Cassie."

Though it was almost exactly what her brother had said last night, she brushed Flynn's comment aside. "I doubt I'll win, but it's still a huge honor to be a finalist."

"Could I see what you made?"

"I had to courier it to Portland for the ceremony."

"How about a picture, then?"

She shouldn't be nervous about show but her heart was pounding a little fas scrolled through the pictures on her pho to him. She had created a three-foot-by-th out of fifty different kinds and colors candy. The overall effect was that of an painting, brushstrokes of pastel colors a canvas.

He stared at the picture without sa for the longest time. "You made *this* out o

She licked her lips. "Yup."

He stared at her as though he couldn was telling him the truth. "It's beautiful, C

His praise sent warmth shooting "Thank you."

It was long past time to continue la dozens of candies for the Town Hall stru mayor's office had commissioned for block party. She turned to wash her han then put on the white apron over her cloth

Though she wasn't sure she'd ever liv Flynn had walked in on—her skin threat beet red every time she thought about it– pleased to see him.

Lola had clearly thought he was here a date. Heck, her sister had practically s since—he'd obviously meant it from a strictly professional standpoint.

Trying to shove away the disappointment when she'd known all along that he was *miles* out of her reach, she asked, "What would you want to know about me?"

"Everything."

His answer took her aback. No one had ever been so interested in her before. Honestly, she still couldn't figure out why he was.

Then something hit her. "Don't all the women in your movies die in a really horrible way?"

He frowned. "You're right, they do, which now that you've pointed it out, is pretty messed up. How about this—what if I promise that the character I base on you won't die?"

She thought about that for a moment. "Not dying is a good start. But I'd like it better if she were actually happy."

He looked uncomfortable for a moment. "I'd like to say I can promise you that. Unfortunately, I don't think I can write *happy* convincingly."

She waited for him to tell her why that was—after all, saying he didn't really understand happiness was pretty huge.

Instead, he simply said, "This is yet another reason why I think who you are, and what you do, could provide some really solid inspiration for my writing."

*Inspiration?* That suddenly seemed a whole lot bigger than just helping him out with some candy-confectioner-from-a-big-family character research.

"Why would you need me to inspire you?" She held out her arms. "I'm just *me*. An open book without dark secrets or hidden mysteries."

"That's *exactly* why I need you." He must have seen that she still didn't get it. "When you're with Ruby, joy radiates from you." He looked uncomfortable again as he said, "The truth is that I haven't felt much joy in my life." His discomfort ratcheted up yet another notch. "I need to understand it. Not just for my screenplay, but for Ruby too. Trust me, your agreeing to work with me on this would be the best thing that could happen." He pinned her with a serious look. "Will you do it, Cassie?"

The hope in his gaze—so uncertain, yet there all the same—had her nodding before she realized it.

"Thank you, Cassie."

She was more than a little shell-shocked that she had just agreed to be an Oscar-winning screenwriter's *inspiration.* But at this moment it was far more important for him to know he was wrong about himself than it was for her to poke into things she could sense that he'd prefer to leave untouched.

"I can maybe understand why you might want to

look at your characters in a different way for your movies, but when it comes to Ruby, you don't need me to teach you how to feel joy."

He stared at her as though she were speaking another language, so she tried to make herself clearer.

"You should hear yourself laugh when she makes a silly face. That laughter comes from the deepest part of your heart. I know it does. It's obvious that you love Ruby with everything you are."

"Of course I love Ruby. She deserves the best of everything—to know joy and hope and the power of real, lasting love."

"So do you." Cassie was so impassioned that, without realizing it, she'd walked around her worktable and reached for his hands. "You deserve to know joy and hope and love, too."

The buzzing of his cell phone had her belatedly realizing that she'd completely invaded his personal space. Jumping back, she smacked her hip on the sharp corner of the stainless-steel countertop.

Hastening back to her workstation, she counted out pieces of the various shapes and colors of her homemade candy while he looked at his phone. "Everything okay?" she asked once he'd slipped it back into his pocket.

"Ruby's doing great." He looked hugely relieved. "Your mom just let me know that they played in the yard with the dog, and then Ruby ate lunch, and now she's settling down for a nap until I come back to pick her up."

"It's okay if you want to pick her up early, you know." Cassie's voice was gentle.

She could see how much he wanted to do just that, even as he said, "All of the baby books say it's important to foster positive time apart."

"There's a big difference between something someone wrote in a book and going literally overnight from being a single, child-free guy, to being responsible for raising a child. It would be a really huge change for anyone to deal with. Don't get me wrong, you're *amazing* with Ruby. Even Ashley thinks so, and she isn't too thrilled with most of your gender. But it's not like you had nine months to prepare for Ruby, or got to sit down with a girlfriend or spouse and talk about whether you wanted to have kids. It must feel like your world has been completely upended."

"I can deal with my world being upended," he said in a low voice. "But I'll never forgive myself if I screw everything up."

"You won't. You *aren't*."

"My parents did."

Though he didn't offer up anything more than that, she sensed he'd just let her into a part of his heart that he rarely shared with anyone.

"I don't know anything about your parents, Flynn. But what I *do* know is that you have created an extraordinary life for yourself regardless of how they raised you. I get that you're nervous about being Ruby's father—"

"I don't even know who the guy is."

"That's just biology. You are her *dad* now."

He sat back on his stool, looking utterly overwhelmed. "*Dad.* I never thought I'd be anyone's dad. That I'd have a little girl to raise and protect...and love." He looked down at the text Cassie's mother had sent, longing written all over his face.

"We can work on your character stuff tomorrow morning. I'll still be here building the Town Hall. But right now, you need to go be with your baby girl. Give her a kiss for me, will you?"

As he raced out of Cassie's workshop to get to her parents' house in what would surely be record time, her heart turned to mush.

# CHAPTER NINE

Flynn spent the next twenty-four hours thinking about his conversation with Cassie. He'd gone to talk about how she was the inspiration for a new character...and yet somehow they'd ended up talking about him.

He'd opened up to her more than he had to anyone else. He'd told her he didn't know the first thing about happiness. He'd admitted that he was terrified about whether he had what it took to raise Ruby well. And he'd confessed that his parents hadn't been good ones.

Only to have her give him the pep talk of all pep talks—and genuinely seem to mean every word.

Flynn had never felt guiltier about being a lying son of a bitch.

The next morning, he and Ruby were up early enough to hit the park in the square before he took her to Beth's. Yesterday afternoon, Flynn had discovered how much Ruby loved being pushed on the swings. No less delighted today, she kicked her feet and clapped her hands with every push.

Sometimes, when Flynn looked at his little girl, he

wasn't sure his heart could withstand the force of his feelings. He'd never known anyone could be so sweet, so pure, so ready to be happy.

Except for Cassie.

He didn't let himself second-guess his urge to make a detour toward Cassie's Confections on the way to Beth's house. He might not be able to give Cassie the truth, but he could at least give her a few minutes with his adorable other half.

Now that Ruby's tooth was in, she was a bundle of joy. All morning, she'd been giggling as she played with Ellie the elephant, then her new striped socks by pulling them off and throwing them across the room, then a beautifully colored leaf that had fallen into her stroller. Everything seemed a wonder to her as she happily played, whether with his participation or independently.

In Los Angeles, they'd both been wary, nervous, anxious. But in Cassie's cabin in the woods, with the forest literally at their doorstep and some time with Beth and the dog at the Sullivan family home, Ruby seemed to have a totally new outlook on life. One that Flynn longed to share with her, if not for his guilt over lying to Cassie—and by extension, her whole family.

They were soon at her office, his heart pounding fast as he rang the bell. Flynn hadn't been this nervous about seeing a woman since he was seventeen and newly arrived in Los Angeles. Already six foot four before he was out of his teens, he hadn't quite filled out by that point, but he'd soon realized that whatever it was women seemed to like, he had. Thirty pounds of muscle later, he'd never had trouble getting a date.

And yet, though he wasn't trying to date Cassie, here he was with sweaty palms and a racing heart.

"Flynn! Ruby!" Cassie beamed at them both as she opened the door, and when she immediately reached down to unbuckle Ruby from the stroller, pick her up, and cuddle her, he wasn't at all surprised. In fact, he would have been surprised if she *hadn't*.

He couldn't help but compare her instinctive need to pepper Ruby with kisses every time she saw the baby to the way his ex had reacted to Ruby. Anja had not only never hugged or kissed Ruby, she had barely looked at her before saying good-bye.

"This is the best surprise ever," Cassie said as she brought Ruby through to her workshop and Flynn followed, leaving the stroller outside. He would never have done that in LA, but he couldn't imagine anyone in Bar Harbor making a run for it with his stroller, no matter how expensive it was.

He couldn't help but continue to make comparisons, this time between Bar Harbor and Los Angeles. Southern California had been a huge step up from the desolate back of nowhere in which he'd grown up, but he'd still been looking over his shoulder in Hollywood, still been on edge, still operated with a base level of suspicion toward everyone around him.

Whereas here in northern Maine, it was starting to sink into his extremely hard head that suspicion would be nothing more than a waste of time. Especially when he had so many Sullivans on his side.

"I thought you might like to see Ruby before I dropped her off with your mom," he said. "And I knew she would be thrilled to see you." *Just like I am.*

"That's so thoughtful of you to bring your sweet little girl to see me." Cassie looked at him as though he'd just given her the world's greatest gift.

When he'd given her diamonds, she'd been horrified and couldn't wait to return them. But she would happily accept the gift of time with Ruby any day of the week.

Something cold inside his heart began to thaw, just from watching Cassie with Ruby as she made the stuffed elephant talk.

*"Ruby,"* she said in her silly Ellie the Elephant voice, *"your eyes shine brighter than any jewel. Your smile is prettier than a rose garden. And your kisses are sweeter than all the candy in the world."*

Ruby giggled, the same delightful sound that he was lucky enough to listen to all day long.

"She's happy." He knew Cassie could see this for

herself, but it felt good to say the words aloud.

"She sure is." Cassie gave Ruby another kiss. "Good job, Dad."

He hadn't been fishing for compliments and still didn't believe them when they came. "It's being with you, and your mom, and getting to live in your cabin and be outside in the woods that's doing it."

"All of that might be helping out a little bit," Cassie replied, "but like I told you yesterday, it's *you* making her happy."

He opened his mouth to argue with her, but her sudden peal of laughter stopped him. Ruby was holding the elephant now, waving it in the air the way Cassie moved the stuffed animal when she made it talk, while making little singsong sounds.

"Look at how smart she is, making Ellie talk and move all on her own!" Cassie exclaimed. "It obviously runs in the family. Just watch, she's going to end up being a brilliant storyteller, just like her daddy."

It was amazing how easily she said the word *daddy*, as though it was unthinkable that Flynn wouldn't have what it took to step up to the plate and be a great father to Ruby.

"If I end up having a story to tell."

"You will." She mimicked the notoriously morose donkey from the children's books in Ruby's bag, obviously poking fun at his response. Flynn couldn't remember the last time anyone had teased him like this. Probably because it had never happened. "After all," she continued, her smile back in place, "you have me to inspire you."

When she laughed again, clearly not taking herself at all seriously, her laughter lit up the same part of his heart that Ruby's giggles did.

Just then, his phone buzzed. Before he could pull it from his pocket, she said, "I'm going to bet that's Mom getting angsty about seeing her little treasure."

He read the message and nodded. "I should take her over now."

"You'll come back, won't you?"

He liked Cassie's obvious desire to spend time with him, more than he should given that she could never be his. But if all he could have was the next few weeks together learning the heart and soul of what made her who she was, he would take it.

"I will. After all," he said with a smile, "I still need to get to know you better."

When she smiled back, he found he couldn't look away from her beautiful face. Another text buzzing in from her mother finally got him back on track, buckling Ruby into her stroller and walking down the street to the Sullivan family home.

★ ★ ★

Cassie's mother and Ruby couldn't have been happier to see each other.

Again, Cassie's father was out, leaving Flynn feeling as though he'd just had his reprieve extended. Flynn wouldn't be surprised if the first time Ethan Sullivan got him alone, Cassie's father sent him out to walk the proverbial plank—and he wouldn't blame him for it either.

He was halfway back to Cassie's office when he passed a flower shop. Her smile was so radiant, he wanted to do whatever he could to make her smile again. Inside, he nearly bought the biggest, showiest bouquet. But then he realized it would be like giving her the diamond bracelet—meant more to impress than to give joy.

He stood studying the flowers for a few minutes. Which ones would Cassie like best? Her candy confections were incredibly colorful. No shrinking violet, his Cassie.

He caught himself a moment too late. She wasn't *his*. She couldn't be *his*.

But he was still going to buy her flowers, damn it.

In the end, his instincts told him to go with an array of bright Gerbera daisies in red, orange, coral, pink, and yellow. The woman at the register asked if he wanted them sent over, but he wanted the pleasure of seeing Cassie's reaction.

Flynn had never walked down any street carrying a bouquet of flowers before. Passers-by smiled at him, the kind of smile you gave a man when you knew he was about to make his sweetheart's day.

If only they knew the truth: that Cassie deserved flowers from a far better man than he. Why was she still single? It was something he didn't understand—one of the many things where she was concerned, actually. There should be men lining up around the block to be with her.

Then again, perhaps he shouldn't be so surprised. Men, in his experience, could be complete idiots.

Once again, he was standing at her office door, his heart pounding a little too fast. These nerves were becoming a regular thing where Cassie was concerned.

He rang the bell, but when she didn't come, and figuring she may have left it unlocked because she knew he was coming back, he decided to try the door. He called out to let her know he was in the building, and he was pleased by how happy she sounded when she told him to come on back.

He wouldn't win any points for wishing he might find her nearly naked again…but that didn't stop him from wishing anyway.

Of course, when he walked into her workshop, she was fully clothed, with the added layer of an apron. Her back was to him as she counted out gumdrops from a jar behind her.

"Flynn, perfect timing! I was just about to—"

Her words fell away as she glanced at him over her shoulder and saw the flowers.

"I bought these for you." He felt like a thirteen-year-old with a crush on the most unattainable girl in school. "I hope you like them."

The candy fell out of her hands as she spun around to take them from him. "Are you kidding? I *love* them." She inhaled their scent, a look of utter bliss on her face.

He half hated himself for a sudden, and rather desperate, fantasy of seeing that blissful look on her face in bed, the sheets tangled around them, her skin flushed and warm beneath him as he made love to her.

"No one has ever bought me flowers before." Her words yanked him from his fantasy, and he realized she was smiling shyly at him. "Thank you, they're beautiful."

*Not nearly as beautiful as you are.*

Selfishly, he was glad that he was the first man ever to give her flowers. After he and Ruby headed back to California, maybe Cassie would think of him whenever she saw daisies.

Because he already knew he wouldn't be able to stop thinking of her.

She filled a tall glass container with water for the flowers. "How did you know Gerbera daisies are my favorite?"

He very nearly punched his fist in the air at having gotten it right. "Everything you make is so bright and colorful—I wanted to find flowers that matched what you do with candy."

She gave him a look he couldn't quite read. "Once I've put these in water, I have to show you something." She was both efficient and delicate as she arranged the flowers in the makeshift vase. Then she wiped her hands and reached for one of the binders on the corner of the counter. She flipped through a few pages, before turning the open page so that he could see it.

He looked at the photo, then up at her in surprise. "You made a confection that looks just like the bouquet."

She nodded. "It's almost as though you had seen it and asked the florist to put together the same custom bouquet."

Flynn had never put much stock in the idea of being so in tune with another person that you could read their mind. And yet, now that Cassie had shown him this picture...

"What did you make this for?"

"Last year, we had a pretty rough winter. I couldn't afford to buy flowers every week, so I decided I'd make a more permanent display." She laughed as she added, "More like semi-permanent, since I kept popping the

petals into my mouth. One day I realized I'd deadhead-
ed all of my candy flowers."

"I've never met anyone like you, Cassie." When
her laughter fell away, he realized how serious his
statement sounded. "I mean that in a good way."

"I've never met anyone like you either." Though
she wasn't smiling as she said it, she added, "I mean
that in a good way too."

"You shouldn't." His words were low. Rough.

"Something you're going to learn about me, if you
haven't figured it out already, is that I don't appreciate
being told what to do." For someone so cheerful, she
had a spine of steel. "I like you, Flynn. So you're just
going to have to get used to it." With that, she gathered up the candy pieces that had scattered on the
counter and went back to work. "Now, should we get
started with your character interview stuff so that you
can nail your new screenplay?"

He was still a good half-dozen steps behind her.
Still trying to process how she could possibly think so
highly of him. Before now, he'd only ever gotten
points for his screenwriting skill—and if he was going
to take it into the gutter, for his skills in the bedroom.
But not only had Cassie never seen one of his movies,
he'd come nowhere near making her cry out with
pleasure.

And yet…she liked him anyway.

Tonight, he'd surely be up pondering this. But for now, she was right—he needed to get to work if he was going to have a prayer of making his deadline. It was time to start his character research.

The prettiest, sweetest, sexiest research he'd ever had the good fortune to do.

"Sure, let's get started." He sat on a stool and pulled out his notebook. "When I'm trying to figure out a character, I ask the same three questions about them: What has happened to turn their world upside down? What are they afraid of? And why don't they think they can conquer that fear to set their world back to rights?"

He let himself enjoy watching her work. She had a dusting of cocoa powder across her cheek, her hair was falling out of its ponytail, and her lips looked like she'd been chewing on them.

In other words, she was perfect.

"What has happened to turn your world upside down, Cassie?"

"Nothing." She laughed at her lightning-quick response. "I warned you—no skeletons. No secrets. Apart from dating a few losers, like most women my age, thankfully there's been nothing truly bad in my life."

Though he wasn't surprised by her answer—he was more glad than anything, because he couldn't stand the thought of her being hurt—he said, "How about we try this from another angle? When was the last time you cried?" And if it turned out that some jerk *had* hurt her, he'd personally go hunt the guy down and tear him limb from limb.

She bit her lip, thinking. "If you really want to know, I watched *Trolls* again, and it made me cry."

"You did?" He thought back to the plot. "Why?"

"Because when the grumpy troll finally opens up his heart to save the happy troll—when he risks facing his own demons for her—it is just *so* beautiful."

His brain spun in circles as he tried to follow. "I want to make sure I have this straight: The last time you were sad, it was because you were *happy*?"

She gave him an I-told-you-so look. "Using me as a character reference is already driving you bonkers, isn't it?"

Maybe he really was going a little crazy. Because instead of being irritated that he couldn't quite understand her responses to his questions, he was more intrigued than ever.

By her unshakable cheeriness.

By her brilliant talent with candy as she created a masterpiece before his eyes.

Not to mention the breathtakingly hot sight of her gorgeous curves the previous morning. He wouldn't forget the sight of those anytime soon.

In his previous life—which was what he'd started calling Los Angeles in his head—he would have scoffed at the entire idea of happy tears.

Tears of rage. Tears of sorrow. Tears of pain. Those were all things he could wrap his head around, emotions he regularly wrote about in his screenplays.

But tears of joy? Tears of laughter? Tears born of so much happiness that they couldn't be contained?

It was entirely new ground for Flynn. Ground he wasn't quite sure how to navigate, but knew he needed to anyway. Otherwise, his stories would forever remain one-dimensional. Obvious. Built to a cookie-cutter pattern.

No wonder he'd had to throw out his draft. At long last, it was time to work outside of the box, time to push himself into new territory.

"What else makes you happy-cry?" he asked.

"A perfect sunset. My mom's slow-cooked corned beef and cabbage. When my entire family is in town and we're all laughing together. Every time I hear about one of my cousins getting engaged, or having a baby. I could keep listing things forever." She smiled. "Your turn."

He shook his head. "I can't think of anything."

"Come on." She looked up from her candy Town Hall as she urged him to think harder about his answer. "Something must move you enough to bring tears to your eyes."

She was right. His knee-jerk response hadn't been honest. It was more that he'd been telling lies like that for so long, he'd come to believe them himself.

If he wanted to write a better screenplay, it might not be enough to dig deep into Cassie's mind, heart, and past.

He might have to dig into his own too.

And then it hit him. "The first time Ruby put her arms around me. Knowing she'd given me her trust." He felt his eyes getting damp just thinking about it. "I knew I loved her. With everything I am, forever and ever."

"She knows a good man when she sees him." Cassie's eyes looked a little glassy now too. "She loves you so much, Flynn. Just as much as you love her."

He was glad when one of the gumdrops rolled across the stainless-steel worktop toward him, because it gave him a few moments to reach for it, pop it into his mouth, and pull himself together.

He picked up his pen and wrote *happy tears* in his notebook. Research had always been one of the easier parts of his job—talking with a cop, interviewing a chef, poring over documents in a library. It had certainly never involved his emotions. And no subject had ever turned his questions back on him.

It was why he was stalling, rather than moving directly to his second question about what she was afraid of. He wasn't a good enough liar to believe that Cassie wasn't going to ask him what *he* was afraid of.

Unsurprisingly, she must have sensed him warring with himself, because without any prompting, she answered his follow-up question. "I'm afraid of something bad happening to my parents, to my siblings, to my cousins and their kids, to my friends." She shook her head. "And since I haven't had much practice dealing with difficult things, I'm afraid that if someone I love did end up hurt in a terrible way, I'd crumble."

"You wouldn't." He knew it with every fiber of his being. "I sure as hell hope everyone important to you stays healthy and happy, but if something bad did happen, you'd be their pillar of strength. Always there with a smile, with laughter that they desperately need, and with the fortitude to keep moving forward even when it might feel easier just to stop."

She had stopped working and was staring at him now. "How can you know that?"

"Same way you always know exactly how I feel about Ruby. In some ways, you're a complete mystery to me, with your happy-crying and your endless love for little animated trolls." Just saying it made his mouth quirk up at the corner. "And still, I get you, Cassie."

"I get you too, don't I, Flynn?"

"You might be just about the only person who does."

# CHAPTER TEN

Cassie was stunned. Not only by the direction in which their conversation had gone, but also by how Flynn seemed to feel their connection as deeply as she did.

Her attraction to him might be one-sided, but at least their budding friendship wasn't.

"Are you going to ask me your third question?" she said.

"No." He closed his notebook.

"Why not?"

"Because I already know that there's no fear you wouldn't be able to conquer."

He was wrong, though.

She was afraid right now.

Afraid he would see that she had already gone beyond simply wanting to be his friend.

Afraid of what would happen if he ever realized just how badly she longed for him to pull her into his arms and kiss her.

"Besides," he continued, "I'd much rather you showed me how to do that."

Her brain had short-circuited somewhere between the moment he'd said she was the only one who understood him and when she started having wild fantasies about kissing him. "How to do what?"

"Build a masterpiece out of candy."

She looked down and realized that even though her head was muddled and befuddled, her hands were still working on the outer walls of the Town Hall building.

"You want to help me build this?"

"I would. But only if I won't get in your way."

She smiled at him. "I'd love the help, Flynn."

Before she could say anything else, her phone buzzed. When she pulled it out of her back pocket, she saw a text from her brother Rory.

*I need your help with something. Can you come by the studio as soon as you get a chance?*

Cassie had been worrying about her brother for a while now. Whatever he needed, she would always be there for him. So though it was terrible timing when Flynn seemed to be opening up to her a little bit, she texted back to let Rory know she'd be there in fifteen minutes.

"Can we take a rain check on the candy-building tutorial until tomorrow? Rory needs me to help him with something."

"Of course." Flynn got off the stool and slung his

computer bag over his shoulder. "I've taken up enough of your time today as it is."

"No." She reached for his hand and wrapped her fingers around his. But though a charge shot through her from that one simple touch, she didn't let go. Not when she wanted so badly for him to know one thing. "I loved spending time with you today."

The next thing she knew, he was tugging her closer, then kissing her on the cheek. "I loved it too."

And then he was gone, leaving her staring after him with her hand on her cheek.

Rory's follow-up text of the thumbs-up icon buzzed her back into motion. She took off her apron, washed the sugar from her hands, loaded several small boxes of candy and baked goods into an oversized bag, and headed out.

Her brother's studio was a couple of blocks farther from the water in a converted warehouse. Eight artists and makers shared the space, which was filled with their individual studios and one large combined working area. Cassie loved to drop by periodically to see what they were working on.

She particularly loved Zara's work designing frames for eyeglasses. Zara was the newest artist in the building, and Cassie had immediately struck up a friendship with her. Before heading to Rory's furniture workshop, which took up the rear of the building,

Cassie popped by Zara's studio.

"Hi, Zara. I hope I'm not disturbing you," she said when her friend looked up. Zara had on a pair of thick-framed green and blue glasses, and from what Cassie could see, she was working on yet another brilliant colorway for a new style of frame. "I thought I'd bring over a refill of your favorites before you ran out." Cassie reached into her bag and pulled out a box filled with multicolored fruit marmalade sweets.

"You must be a mind reader." Zara got up to give Cassie a hug, then happily accepted the candy box. "I was about to eat my last ones today. It was literally giving me heart palpitations."

Cassie laughed. "I know how busy you are." With every pair of custom glasses Zara sold, she gave away a pair. As she was still growing her business and doing all her own manufacturing and shipping, at present there were easily two dozen boxes on the table in the corner that looked ready to go out. "Anytime you need more sugar from me, you should take a page from Rory's book—he just texted and said he needed my help with something, which I'm almost positive is actually a request for candy and cupcakes."

Zara's smile fell away. "Your brother should get his own damned candy if he needs it so badly."

*Hmmm.* From what Cassie could tell, there had been sparks between Zara and Rory from the beginning. Sparks that neither of them had any intention of acknowledging. On the surface, it seemed they didn't much like each other, but Cassie had never seen her brother react to a woman in quite the way he did with Zara, even with the serious girlfriend he used to have. Almost as though Zara had gotten under his skin...and he didn't know what to do about it.

"What did he do now?" Cassie asked.

"He's been stomping around this morning like a bear with a thorn up his—"

"Cassie?" Rory suddenly appeared in the doorway, interrupting their conversation. "Why didn't you come straight back to my workshop?"

Before Cassie could respond, Zara said, "Because your sister is a nice person who stops to say hello to a friend, instead of dashing to your side every time you request her presence from your throne."

He scowled at Zara. "Still pissed I drank the rest of the coffee, huh?"

She scowled back. "The coffee? You think that's the only reason I'd be pissed at you? How about when you—" She broke off in mid-sentence. "Sorry, Cassie. You don't need to be in the middle of this. I can tear your brother apart later."

"Is that a promise?" he drawled.

Zara gave him the one-fingered salute, then turned back to Cassie. "Thanks again for the candy. You're the best."

Rory's muscles and good looks tended to turn most women's knees to mush. Only Zara was a holdout when it came to Cassie's brother.

Then again, could the sparring simply be her way of keeping her real feelings for him at bay? Because if the two of them started dating, it would be absolutely *glorious* to have a woman like Zara, who didn't take nonsense from anyone, to keep Rory in line.

As Cassie and Rory walked together to his studio, she debated whether to say anything about her brother's rather sparky repartee with Zara. But given that she hadn't appreciated his weighing in on her situation with Flynn, she decided to keep her thoughts to herself. For now anyway. For all his bravado, she wasn't sure Rory was totally happy.

Could Zara help with that? And was he even ready for a new relationship?

Still mulling those questions over, Cassie asked, "What are you working on today?"

"My client asked for a contemporary inlay pattern, which I've sketched out." He'd done a great job of creating a twelve-by-twelve mosaic that could have come straight out of Frank Lloyd Wright's sketchbook. "But when I started cutting and laying out the various shades and shapes of wood, it didn't look right."

She studied the pattern for a while. "What if you

swapped these golden strips for the dark red squares?"

He shifted the pieces around, then nodded. "That's it." He grinned at her. "I've been staring at this for days, when I should have just called you."

"Happy to help."

"About that. I asked Rafe to do a little digging into your new friend."

"You called Rafe?" She was the one scowling now. "That's low, even for you. How dare you ask our cousin to dig through Flynn's business?"

"It's not all bad," Rory replied, as though that got him off the hook for being a prying, nosy, pain-in-the-butt big brother. "Turns out Flynn has given a boatload of money to children's charities over the years."

"And you're surprised?" She was furious now. "Flynn is a good man. Which you would have realized if you'd bothered to speak civilly to him at dinner last night."

"Look, I'm sorry if you think this is none of my business—"

"It *is* none of your business!" Rory had gone too far this time. *Way* too far. "I would never dream of hiring a private investigator to investigate the women *you* go out with."

Rory's eyebrows went up. "So you admit you *are* going out with him."

"No!" She flat-out yelled the word. "But that's irrelevant. Flynn and Ruby are guests in my cabin—and friends of Smith—and I would hope my family would go out of their way to make them feel welcome, not treat them like criminals."

"Of course Ruby isn't a criminal. She's only a baby. Flynn, on the other hand—Rafe said there are things in his file that don't add up."

Cassie put her hands over her ears. "I already told you I don't want to hear it."

"Who wouldn't want to know the dirt on a guy before they make the mistake of hooking up with him?"

"Seriously," Cassie muttered, "it's like talking to a brick wall. No wonder Zara wants to throttle you."

"She said that?"

"No, she didn't say that. I'm just guessing that's what she must feel given how annoying and insufferable and provoking you always are." She picked up her bag. "If I were petty, I would take back the candy and cupcakes I brought you."

His face lit up. "You brought me treats?"

"Here." Cassie gave him the goodies. "But you'd better promise to keep your nose out of Flynn's business from now on. Whatever he wants me to know, he'll tell me if and when he's ready."

His phone rang before he could reply. "I've been waiting for this call. Thanks for the help, sis." He gave her a kiss on the forehead, then walked away before she could press him for his promise to back off.

* * *

Flynn tucked the baby monitor into the back pocket of his jeans, then headed outside to gather the hand saw, hammer, and nails that he and Ruby had picked up earlier at the hardware store. The monitor's signal reached a good ten yards around the cabin, and he could hear her soft snuffles as she settled down for her afternoon nap.

She'd had a great time with Beth that morning and hadn't fought going down for a nap a few hours later. Flynn knew he should probably get a couple of hours of writing in. But not only were his new story ideas still completely murky, there was something else he wanted to do first.

The flower boxes on the front of Cassie's cottage were rotting. Given how thrilled she'd been by the bouquet he'd brought her that morning, he figured it had to bother her that her flower boxes were the only thing on her property not in top shape.

Normally, he would have used a power saw and screw gun to do the work, but he didn't want to risk waking Ruby during her nap. It was one of the first things he'd learned immediately upon bringing Ruby home: Waking a sleeping baby was a *seriously* bad idea.

Fortunately, there were two sawhorses and a sheet of plywood in the shed, which Flynn set up near the front door. After lifting out the flower pots, he carefully removed the boxes from beneath the window, confirming that they were ready for the fire when the wood crumbled in his hands.

With his new tape measure, he took the measurements, then picked up one of the cedar boards he'd purchased at the hardware store. Though he hadn't done much woodworking over the past twenty years, the skills came back pretty quickly. After making a few early mistakes—measure twice, cut once—he hit his stride, and soon he'd made the first new flower box of the four he needed to replace.

He was hanging it beneath the left-most window when he heard a car coming up the long driveway. Though he'd left her workshop only this morning, did Cassie long to see him again as much as he'd been longing to see her?

But she didn't drive a big black SUV. Immediately, his radar for trouble went up.

Flynn had been extra careful since arriving in Bar Harbor with Ruby. Apart from visiting Cassie's workshop, he had only been to the Sullivan Café and to the hardware store. At the café, he'd sat out of sight in the back corner. And he'd worn his baseball cap and dark glasses to the hardware store today.

Had someone still been able to figure out who he was? Had they alerted the press? Was this a car full of paparazzi angling for the big scoop and the big payout, the same way his nanny had?

He cursed, already furious at whoever it was. Ruby had only just begun to settle in, and Flynn not only didn't want to move her again, he also realized he didn't want to fall into the pattern of always being on the run.

Ruby deserved a home. A real home of the kind he'd never had himself.

Every muscle in Flynn's body was tense as the SUV came to a stop, and the door opened. Perhaps it should have been a relief to see Cassie's brother Rory step out, rather than the paparazzi.

But it wasn't. Not when Rory looked like he meant business.

The kind of business where he eviscerated the guy thinking about getting into his sister's pants.

Rory looked at Flynn, then scanned the area around him. "Where's Ruby?"

"Napping."

"My nephew wasn't much of a napper at Ruby's age," Rory said in a deceptively easy voice. "Ashley was pretty much a zombie for those first couple of years."

Flynn could have responded in just as easy a tone, but he knew Cassie's brother hadn't come to make small talk. "Something I can help you with?"

Instead of answering, Rory gestured to Flynn's project. "You're replacing Cassie's flower boxes?"

The look of surprise on her brother's face was borderline insulting. Scratch that—there was no borderline about it. "They're rotting."

Rory nodded. "I've been meaning to make new ones for her." He went to take a closer look at the box Flynn had just screwed to the front of the house. "Not bad."

Flynn had done a little research into Cassie's siblings since he'd met them at dinner. The furniture Rory made was mightily impressive. A *not bad* from him was a massive compliment.

"Where'd you learn to do woodwork?" Rory asked.

"I grew up in the woods. There were always projects." Projects that, as a teenager, Flynn had to learn to take care of to keep their home from completely falling down around them.

"I find a lot of the materials for my furniture in Cassie's woods," Rory told him.

"But that's not why you're here this afternoon, is it?"

"Nope." But as Rory moved away from the house, all he said was, "I'll help you build the rest of the flower boxes. You'll be done by the time Ruby wakes up."

Though Flynn could easily guess that Cassie's brother was simply biding his time until he went after him, he wasn't going to refuse his help. Flynn wanted to surprise Cassie with four new flower boxes the next time she came to the cabin. He'd even bought fresh flowers for them, just as bright and sunshiny as she was.

He almost laughed at himself. *Sunshiny* wasn't a word that had ever been in his vocabulary.

Not until he'd met Cassie.

In silence, the two men cut and hammered together the new boxes. When they were done forty-five minutes later, they planted the flowers in fresh potting soil, then stood back to look over their work.

"Looks good," Rory said.

"I appreciate the help."

"You didn't need it." Rory ran a hand over his hair, looking uncomfortable. "My cousin is a private investigator. I asked him to look into you."

Flynn braced himself. "And?"

"You're very charitable," Rory said first. "Apart from your large donations and the details of your career and the women you've dated, he didn't find much. After he and I talked this morning, I was planning to come after you to convince you to tell me what you're hiding." Rory had big enough muscles that if things got physical, Flynn would have to work like crazy to hold his ground. "But I'm thinking of giving that a pass."

Nothing could have surprised Flynn more. "What's stopping you?"

"Cassie asked me to lay off." Rory half laughed as he said, "More like yelled it, actually."

Though he was surprised to hear that Cassie could yell about anything, Flynn said, "You agreed?"

"Not at first. I was thinking it was up to me to make sure she didn't get hurt by some slick star from Hollywood who wouldn't have a clue how to treat her right." He looked Flynn up and down in his T-shirt and worn jeans, covered in sweat and sawdust. "You're less slick than you seem at first glance."

Again, an unexpected compliment. "You still don't trust me, though, do you?"

"Nope." Rory wasn't at all apologetic about it. "Cassie is as nice as they come, and I'm not just saying that because she's my sister. She's a sister who will drop everything for you. A daughter who would never willingly hurt her parents. And a friend who will go out of her way to make you happy. Her heart is so damned big that she can't help but want to be there for everyone." Rory pinned him with a hard look. "I sure as hell hope you're not planning on taking advantage of her."

"Of course not." Regardless of Flynn's fascination with her, he knew someone so good, so pure of heart, could never be his. "Cassie deserves only the best."

Rory studied him before nodding. "Just wanted to make sure we're clear about that."

A soft cry from Ruby came through on the monitor.

"Mind if I come in and get some water?" Rory asked as Flynn turned to head inside.

"Help yourself." He went into Ruby's room and picked her up out of her crib. She was a little sweaty from her nap, and he brushed her damp curls from her forehead.

He handed over Ellie the elephant, her favorite stuffed animal, then carried her out on his hip while she made Ellie dance in the air.

Rory was finishing his drink when they came into the kitchen. Putting the glass down, he smiled at Ruby. "Cute kid."

She beamed at him, then reached out her arms for him to take her. Clearly, she was a sucker for a good-looking face. Flynn made a mental note to teach her to be on her guard against guys like Rory when she got older. Guys who were too good-looking, too charming, too talented for their own good.

It wasn't hard for Flynn to guess that part of the reason Cassie's brother was so worried about Flynn hurting her was because Rory didn't have the best track record with women himself. Still, her brother didn't balk at holding the baby.

"What's that you've got in your hand?" Rory asked

her, touching the stuffed elephant's trunk.

Ruby made her funny little noises as she danced it around in front of Rory's face.

"Cassie christened it Ellie the elephant," Flynn told him.

"Sounds like something my sister would come up with."

As Ruby cracked herself up, Rory smiled at her again. "You're going to be a little heartbreaker, aren't you?"

As if to back up his remark, she puckered her lips for a kiss.

Laughing, he gave her a little peck on the lips before handing her back to Flynn and heading out.

A few minutes later, as Flynn settled Ruby on his lap to feed her a post-nap bottle, he remarked, "That didn't go the way I expected it to." Especially after Rory had told him he'd hired a private investigator, which ranked right up there as one of Flynn's worst nightmares.

For nearly twenty years, he'd lived his life within the framework he'd come up with on a Greyhound bus at seventeen—change who he was, make a lot of money, be lauded as a professional success. But for the past several weeks, nothing had fit within that framework.

And suddenly, he found himself wondering if that might not be such a bad thing.

# CHAPTER ELEVEN

Cassie had worked late the previous day to get her Town Hall candy structure to a point where Flynn would best be able to help her. Fortunately, hard work was also a good way to get rid of her anger at her brother and cousin for investigating him.

Cassie didn't get mad very often, but when she did, everyone knew to watch out.

She'd sent texts to both Rory and Rafe telling them to put anything they'd found out about Flynn through a shredder—*or else*. Rafe had sent a video of the papers going into his shredder, which made her smile in spite of herself. And Rory had texted back early in the evening with one word: *Sorry*.

By the time Flynn rang her office doorbell the next morning, she had icing ready to go in the piping bags, along with the various piles of candy that would create the brick walls.

She went to open the door. "Good morning. Come on in." It was hard to speak normally after losing her breath, but she hoped she'd pulled it off. Surely at some point she'd be used to Flynn's looks—and the force of her reaction to him. "How's Ruby doing today?"

"As excited as ever to hang with your mom and the dog."

She smiled, glad Flynn seemed to be feeling better about allowing someone else to watch Ruby for a few hours in the mornings. She couldn't imagine how difficult it would be to trust another caregiver after what his Hollywood nanny had pulled. It was beyond her how people could behave in such a horrible way— to even *think* of selling a story of two people who had suffered such great loss.

"Ready to become a master candy builder?" she asked.

His smile was another breath-stealer. "I'll do my best."

Cassie could easily guess that Flynn was nothing less than a perfectionist with his screenplays. You didn't get to where he was without being both a brilliant artist and dedicated to putting in the hours to make your work the best it could be.

"Okay, wash your hands and then I'll put you to work."

Just washing his hands, Flynn was far sexier than any man she'd ever known, with his broad shoulders and well-muscled limbs. How he stayed so fit when he sat behind a computer writing all day, she couldn't imagine.

"Do you play sports?" she found herself asking before she could swallow the words.

He turned off the faucet and grabbed a hand towel to wipe off his hands before turning to her. "I play basketball with a group of guys at the gym in LA. Why?"

Her mouth went dry as she was hit with a potent vision of Flynn in shorts and a T-shirt, all sweaty and fierce while he worked out. "I was just thinking that you look really fit."

Slowly, he scanned her curves. "So do you. What's your workout of choice?"

*Sex with you.*

Oh God. She hadn't just said that out loud, had she?

Thankfully, there was no look of shock on his face. Which meant she had shouted the words only inside her own head.

He was still waiting for her response, so she said, "I love to hike in Acadia National Park."

He smiled. "Ruby seems to be a fan of hiking already. As soon as she sees me get out the carrier backpack to walk around your property, she claps her hands."

She was about to respond when he moved beside

her. Close enough that she could smell his scent—fresh, clean pine with a hint of spice.

"Show me how you make magic, Cassie."

She hoped he couldn't see that she was trembling slightly as she picked up a handful of handmade candy bricks and dropped them into his palm. "The key is to work quickly enough that the frosting between the bricks for the wall doesn't quite set, but not so quickly that it squirts out between the pieces."

He shot her a surprised look. "You're going to let me work on your Town Hall? I figured you'd set me up in the corner with a smaller project that you could throw into the trash once I'm done with it."

"It isn't rocket science—or putting together a complicated plot for a movie that will thrill millions of people around the world. It's just making one small move forward, again and again, to get to where you need to be. I've always felt like anything is possible if I just remember that."

She piped in some white icing for the mortar between the bricks, placed one of the candies on top of it, then piped in more icing where Flynn would place his piece. "Now you try it."

But he didn't move. "I don't want to damage your work."

"I have faith in you not to let my walls crumble." When that didn't seem to convince him, she said,

"Would it help you get the feel for it if I put my hand over yours and did it with you?"

"Good idea."

When she made the suggestion, she hadn't been thinking about what it would be like to actually touch Flynn. But as she reached out to put her hand over his, she found her breath going again. And when she finally made contact, the back of his hand under her palm, his fingers strong and his skin warm beneath hers, just that tiny little touch affected her so deeply she felt her entire body heat up.

How had she never realized just how intimate it was to touch a man's hand?

Every cell in her body jumped to sensual life as she ran her fingers down his so that they could grasp the piece of candy together. Together, they lifted the piece and moved it toward the wall. Gently, but confidently, she placed the piece beside the one she'd put down a minute ago. It fit perfectly.

"How did that feel to you?" Her voice was huskier than normal.

He turned to meet her eyes again. "It felt just right."

She stared at him, unable to look away. "Do you want to try it yourself this time?"

"Not yet." Was it her imagination, or did his voice have a slightly raw tone? "Show me again, Cassie. Just like that."

Before she could stop it, her brain ran away with her. *Show me again, Cassie. Just like that.* But instead of saying it to her in her workshop, she pictured him saying it in bed. While they were naked, and she was giving in to the sensual urges she'd had since the first moment she'd set eyes on him.

She had to tear herself from her daydream. "Okay." She gestured for him to pick up the piping bag. "We'll start with the mortar. Piping is deceptive. You have to be gentle with it...and yet not be afraid to show it that you know what you're doing."

She should have been prepared to touch him this second time, but if anything, her reaction was even stronger. As though she was already primed to crave the feel of his skin, his heat, his strength. Compared to Flynn, every man she'd been with before seemed no more than a callow boy.

It probably took them only five seconds to ice the wall, but they were officially the five sexiest seconds of Cassie's life. Especially when she realized that Flynn had *exactly* the right touch.

Would it be the same if he were touching *her*?

She'd never wanted to know an answer more. Which was why she made herself drop his hand and say, "I think you're ready to put the next piece on yourself." She prayed that her face wouldn't give away just how much being close to him was affecting her as she added, "I can tell that you're a natural."

His eyes seemed to grow even darker. "If you believe in me, I won't let you down." He turned his focus back to the wall and, in one deft move, had the candy in place.

"It's perfect." But she wasn't looking at the candy structure anymore. She couldn't look away from his face.

"Cassie—" He stared at her, his eyes even darker now, a sinfully beautiful pool of blue from which she couldn't look away.

*Oh God, what was he going to say to her?*

Her doorbell buzzed, utterly obliterating the moment. "Cassie," a woman's voice called out, "I need you to try on the dress again."

"Lola's here." Cassie instinctively moved away from Flynn. Otherwise, her sister was bound to start imagining things about the two of them again.

All the things Cassie could no longer deny that she so badly wanted...

# CHAPTER TWELVE

Lola and Ashley arrived together, as it turned out.

"Hello again, Flynn." Yet again, Lola looked straight out of a fifties photo shoot, from her hair to her makeup and clothes. "We thought we might find you here."

"How's Ruby doing?" Ashley asked.

"Really well. She loves spending time with your mom."

"Kevin was the same way as a baby. Even at ten, he loves spending time with his grandma. And he hasn't stopped talking about Ruby. I've never seen him with a baby before. He obviously can't resist her."

"That's because she's irresistible," Cassie put in.

"I agree that Ruby is the sweetest little girl—and I hate to interrupt our baby lovefest—but I've got a dress to finish." She shot a look at Cassie. "Why are you still dressed?"

"Because I'm not going to try it on in here."

"No need to be shy." She winked at Flynn, then said, "After all, we've all seen you in your underwear."

Barely stifling a groan, Cassie grabbed the dress from her sister and took it through to her office. Lola followed her, leaving Flynn and Ashley alone in the workshop.

"How is your screenplay coming along now that Mom is watching Ruby for a few hours in the morning?" Ashley asked.

He didn't know what Cassie had told them about her participation in his project. "I've decided to start again from scratch. Cassie has agreed to help me, actually."

Ashley raised an eyebrow. "I didn't know Cassie had gotten into the screenplay business."

Though Cassie had told him that her sister liked him, he sensed a wariness in her statement, one he couldn't fault. Cassie's family *should* be wary of a guy like him.

"I'm fleshing out some new character studies." He gestured to the half-built Town Hall. "It's hard not to be inspired by what your sister does." Even a cynic like him could almost believe that anything was possible when Cassie said it.

"She's amazing," Ashley agreed. She gestured to Cassie's work in progress. "I can't even begin to imagine how she does it."

"She was actually letting me put some of the pieces on when you walked in."

Ashley's expression shifted from wary to downright shocked. "Are you telling me she let you not only touch her work, but actually help too?" When he nodded, she shook her head as though she couldn't believe it. "She *never* lets any of us help. Not even Mom."

He wasn't surprised to hear that Cassie was possessive of her work. He was exactly the same way. This was the first time he had ever let anyone be a part of his process.

It was, he realized, not only that he was inspired by what she did. It was also that he trusted her.

Trusted her in a way he had never really trusted anyone else.

If that was how she felt about him too, he was humbled. And confused.

What could he possibly have done to earn that much of her trust?

"You must really be special, Flynn."

"I'm not."

"I had a feeling you were going to say that. But the thing is, my sister is a great judge of character. She was dead-on about Kevin's worthless father and also about every one of the guys Lola has gone out with. Though I'm usually inclined to reserve judgment, if Cassie thinks you're one of the good ones, I'm going to trust her."

"Cassie and I don't—"

He had been about to say they didn't know each other very well, but it was a lie he couldn't tell. They might not have known each other very long, but that didn't diminish the strength of their connection.

A connection that, amazingly, was already stronger than any he'd ever had with anyone else.

"Cassie deserves the best," he said. Flynn wanted Ashley to understand that he would never hurt her sister. That it was the very last thing he would ever want to do. "Someone worthy of her. Someone who understands how amazing she is. Someone who will support her in everything. Someone who will give her a family like the one you all have."

"It doesn't sound like you're putting yourself in the running," Ashley said. "Honestly, I find that pretty surprising."

Despite how uncomfortable Flynn was with Ashley's forthright comments, he couldn't help but respect her for speaking her mind. Beth and Ethan Sullivan had raised their daughters in a way he hoped he could raise Ruby—to stand up for what they believed in, to support the people they loved, and not to back down from difficult discussions.

Though she hadn't asked him a direct question, he knew she was expecting a response. "It's an honor just to be Cassie's friend and learn from her while I'm here."

Raised voices sounded from the office, then Lola came into the workshop, dragging Cassie reluctantly behind her.

"Cassie thinks the dress is too revealing. What do you guys think?"

*"You're gorgeous."*

The words were out of Flynn's mouth before he could stop them. Cassie was beautiful in her regular clothes. She'd been incredibly sexy when he'd walked in on her in her bra and panties. But in the silk and lace dress, with a dusting of sugar across her cheek and icing in her hair, she was *breathtaking*.

"See?" Lola looked victorious. "I told you my dress looks amazing. You've got to get over your need to swaddle yourself in aprons all the time, and let out the goddess you've been hiding."

Cassie closed her eyes in obvious mortification. "I'm not hiding anything, Lola. I just don't want to show up to the awards ceremony looking like I'm interested in getting a piece of anything other than cake."

"The dress is elegant, Cassie," Ashley agreed. "You don't have anything to be worried about."

"Do you think I would send you off in anything but my best?" Lola asked. "When you win—" She held up her hands to forestall Cassie's protests that her win wasn't a sure thing. "—and they release pictures of you with your trophy, everyone is going to look at those pictures and want to know who you're wearing. And," she added a beat later, "they'll be impressed with your confection, of course."

Though Cassie had looked like she wanted to strangle her sister earlier, now she just laughed. "I'm going to change out of this before I get it dirty."

When Cassie left to change, Lola stayed behind this time. "I hope Ash was grilling you while we were gone."

He shook his head, knowing it could have been much worse. "She went easy on me."

"Well, we can't have that, can we?" Lola pinned him with a serious look. "We have sixty seconds before Cassie comes back. That's just enough for me to tell you that if you do anything to hurt my sister, I will personally come hunt you down."

He might be six foot four with a black belt in karate, but he wouldn't want to face down a furious Lola Sullivan. "I feel exactly the same way. If anyone ever hurt her…" Just thinking of it made his chest clench.

She nodded toward the flowers. "Looks like you've already realized that she'd much rather have flowers than diamonds." She graced him with a smile. "I have high hopes for you."

Cassie walked in on the tail end of Lola's sentence,

looking between the two of them. "What are you hoping for, Lola?"

"Ash and I have to run. Flynn will tell you."

Thirty seconds later, they were alone again. Cassie studied his face. "They were saying embarrassing things, weren't they?"

"No." He envied her, having so many people in her corner—including him. After he left Bar Harbor, he'd do his best, even from afar, to make sure no one ever hurt her. "Your sisters are great."

"I agree, they are. But that doesn't mean they won't stick their noses in where they don't belong. What did they say to you?"

"Just that they want you to be happy."

She obviously didn't believe that was the full extent of it. "Please tell me they didn't ask what your intentions toward me are?"

When he didn't immediately deny it, she dropped her head into her hands and groaned.

"Cassie." He moved closer so that he could move her hands away from her face. "They can see that I like you. A lot." Even now, just holding her hands was enough to start a fire burning inside him. "And I think they can also see that I'm not goo—"

Her mouth was on his before he could finish his sentence. Soft and warm and oh so sweet.

When she drew back, her cheeks were flushed, and

there was something akin to shock on her face.

"I didn't mean to do that. I just couldn't stand to hear you say you're not good enough for me—and that was the fastest way I could think of to stop you. But I know better than to assume that you feel that way about me."

She was about to take a step back when he put his hands on her shoulders to keep her close. "You know I damn well do. Hell, that kiss should have taken away any and all doubts. The chemistry that you and I have—it's like nothing I've ever felt." He'd never wanted anything so much in his life as he wanted to kiss her again. "But there are things you don't know about me. Things no one knows." Only his sister had known the truth, and she was gone now.

"One day," Cassie said in a soft voice, "I hope you'll feel that you can trust me enough to tell me those things and finally get them off your chest. But I don't need to know anything more than what I see in your eyes when you're with Ruby." She had so much trust and faith in him, he was awed by it. "And when you're looking at me the way you are right now, even if you obviously don't think you should kiss me again."

No one in Hollywood would have dared speak so plainly. But Cassie would never lie. He knew that with perfect certainty.

He lifted his hand to her cheek, stroking her skin

with the tips of his fingers. "You've already given me so much more than I ever expected to find. You're right that I can't let myself kiss you again. But selfishly, I can't help wanting to spend more time with you anyway."

She looked like she was going to argue with him. But then she said only, "Given that I sprang that kiss on both of us, I think it might be wise to put it on a back burner for a little while. Besides, I've still got plenty to show you—if you're still interested in learning about me for your research, that is."

He'd forgotten all about his screenplay. What if he was as honest as she was? What if he told her his interest in learning about her had a million times more to do with simply wanting to be near her than it had to do with his work?

Instead, what came out of his mouth was, "What are you planning to show me next?"

Her smile widened. "The way I figure it, if you're going to create a character inspired by me, you should experience the things that bring me the most joy. Will it work with Ruby's nap schedule to come by the cabin at two p.m. tomorrow? I want to take you both to my favorite hiking trail."

He was amazed, yet again, at how easily she was able to move from serious to smiling. Everyone he knew in LA loved to wallow in their tortured souls.

Cassie hadn't denied that he might indeed be tortured, but she didn't spend much time focusing on it. Instead, she simply turned her attention back to joy. Just as she had from the moment he'd met her and she'd been so joyful when meeting Ruby.

"Two o'clock should work great."

"Good. Now wash your hands again, and we'll get back to work."

Heat continued to linger in the wake of their spontaneous kiss—as did the weight of their subsequent conversation about it. And yet, there was still a Town Hall to be built from candy. It was nice to have something concrete, something solid and real, to focus on. And to have a reason to work beside Cassie for a little while longer.

"Here's my building plan." She slid over a detailed architectural drawing that showed how each piece fitted together. "You'll probably still be working on your section of the wall by the time you head off to pick up Ruby, but I thought you would like to see how all the little pieces add up to make the whole."

It was the second thing she'd said today that gave him pause. First, that one small move after another was all you really needed to get where you wanted to go. And now, a reminder that big things were usually made up of tiny little pieces.

She had a knack for making the scary seem not

nearly as frightening. The impossible, possible.

He'd always thought big parts of him were irreparably broken, not only because of how he'd been raised, but also because of the countless lies he'd told to rise up out of the trash heap. For the first time, he wondered if it was possible to take one little step, and then another, and another, toward real happiness. And, if he was really stretching, love.

An eighties boy band singing about love broke through his musings.

Before he could ask, Cassie said, "I find pop music helps me when I'm working on something repetitive like this wall. The cheesier the better." She shimmied her hips to the chorus, but her face was a picture of concentration as she laid in more candy along the top edge of the wall. "Do you ever listen to music while you're working?"

He got to work alongside her. "Never."

"That doesn't sound like much fun."

"Writing has rarely been fun for me."

"Then why do you do it?"

"Because it's the one thing I'm good at."

She shot him a disbelieving look. "You're good at kissing. Although, hopefully, you find that to be a heck of a lot more fun."

His hand stilled over his piece of the candy wall. "Two things, then." Though he knew it would be a very bad idea to kiss her again when he couldn't offer her the perfect happy-ever-after that she deserved, he couldn't resist adding, "You're good at it too."

She didn't say anything else, but she didn't need to.

Her smile said it all.

# CHAPTER THIRTEEN

Flynn usually wrote in the afternoons. Now, however, afternoons were the time of day when Ruby was the most active. And he loved the time he spent with Ruby. Whether reading to her from the picture books he'd picked up at the library, or taking her for a walk in the woods, or heading down to the waterfront and splashing around with her—every moment was precious.

Sure, there were sometimes tears when she got hot, or tired, or needed a diaper change, but he admired how easily she could let her emotions out. Even as a very young child, he hadn't been able to do that. Not when his parents had been so unpredictable. All his life, he'd hidden his true thoughts and feelings.

Until Cassie Sullivan came into his life…and started to turn everything inside him upside down.

Sitting on his lap, Ruby gave a huge yawn. It was seven p.m. and they were reading an interactive version of *The Wheels on the Bus* where she could pull on paper tabs to make the wheels turn or the windshield wipers move. He'd never sung in front of anyone before, but with Ruby he was more than happy to sing the song as many times as she wanted him to.

"Are you ready for bed?"

She leaned against his chest and stuck her thumb in her mouth. In her other hand, she held her favorite stuffed elephant.

Flynn's heart was so full that he was sure it must be close to bursting. "We're going to have a big day out with Cassie tomorrow," he told Ruby. "She's going to take us hiking."

At the sound of Cassie's name, Ruby made a little happy sound. As though she was saying, *I really like Cassie. We should see more of her.*

Flynn felt the same way. The more of Cassie he could get into their lives, the happier he and Ruby would be.

He didn't want to think of what it would be like when they were back in California and Cassie was nearly three thousand miles away. Honestly, he didn't like to think about going back to LA at all—back to his expensive but charmless house, to friends who weren't really friends, to a world where people lied to your face without a shred of guilt.

He was pulled out of his dark musings by the press of soft little lips against his. Ruby's hands were on his cheeks, and she was staring into his eyes, looking wise beyond her years. And then she gave him the biggest, sweetest smile.

He smiled back—how could he not?—then kissed her. "You and Cassie have a lot in common. She always knows just what to do to make me smile when I'm acting like a grumpy donkey."

Ruby wrapped her arms around his neck as he got up from the couch to take her to her crib. Though he'd love having her sleep in his room, he'd forced himself to put her into her own bedroom, which she'd been fine with. *He* was the one missing her, wishing he could wake up in the middle of the night and know that he wasn't alone, that there was at least one person he could count on to be there with him in the morning, no matter what.

Gently, he laid her in her crib, tucking a soft blanket over her. "I love you, Ruby."

She smiled at him, then closed her eyes and fell asleep with Ellie the elephant cradled in the crook of one arm.

He watched her for a while before heading back out to the living room. With the long, quiet evening stretching ahead of him, he should use the time to get to work on a new script.

Flynn had never been the kind of writer who procrastinated or suffered from writer's block. On the contrary, his stories had always been the perfect place to escape from the real world.

These past three weeks, it had been a shock to try to chase down the words, only to have them be just out of reach. He'd told himself that his lack of progress was down to being so shell-shocked by the changes in his life, from adjusting to a baby's sleep schedule, and his grief over losing his sister.

But tonight he could no longer tell himself those lies. In Cassie's cabin in the woods, he finally faced that for the past nearly twenty years he hadn't been lying to just everyone else—he'd been lying to himself too.

Lying about feeling happy.

Lying about having everything he wanted.

Even lying about the kind of stories he wanted to tell.

As a child, he'd been so full of darkness, so full of fear. All he'd had to do was bring his nightmares to life. It was as much as he'd ever been willing to share of himself on the page, and no one in the film industry had ever asked him for anything more.

Suddenly, he couldn't stop wondering what kind of story he would tell if he were actually honest. If he stepped out of the dark corners for once—taking a page from Cassie's book by switching from dread and doubt to laughter.

Did he even have it in him to write a movie where his characters *laughed*?

There was only one way to find out.

He was about to sit in front of his laptop on the kitchen table when he remembered how joyful Cassie had been dancing to cheesy pop songs in her workshop. No surprise, the retro fifties-style radio on the kitchen island was already tuned to a station playing eighties music. "Take on Me" came on—the same song that Cassie had been dancing to in her workshop. It felt like a sign that maybe, just maybe, having fun while writing might not be completely out of his reach.

Still, his heart was pounding as he opened his laptop. For the past three weeks, the blinking cursor had been taunting him, daring him to write something, anything. Tonight, however, Flynn was surprised to find the words spilling from his fingertips on the keyboard before the cursor could begin its taunts.

> *Ellie the elephant is born in a factory in upstate New York. She has many brothers and sisters who look like her, with pink stitching along the undersides of their snouts, green on their feet, yellow on their big floppy ears, and bright pink and purple polka dots covering the rest.*
>
> *After each elephant comes to life, they are given a destination. One of Ellie's sisters asks her, "Where are they sending you?"*
>
> *"To a little boy in Centertown." Ellie is full of eager anticipation. "I'm going to show him how to*

*laugh."*

*One of Ellie's brothers asks, "How are you going to do that?"*

*"I'm going to remind him that he already knows how to laugh," Ellie replies. "He's just forgotten for a little while."*

Flynn stared in surprise at the words on his screen.

It was tempting to delete the deeply personal words, to pretend he'd never written them, to return to the tried-and-true thriller format.

But he couldn't do it.

Not when it suddenly felt as though far more was at stake than just a finished screenplay.

# CHAPTER FOURTEEN

Cassie had never felt like this before. Happy and nervous. Excited and scared. Full of anticipation, but also worried.

She'd never fallen for anyone before either.

It wasn't just one person she had fallen for—it was two. She wanted both Flynn *and* Ruby in her life. If things didn't work out for them in Maine and they left, she would not only lose one person she cared deeply for, she'd lose both of them.

Just thinking about it made her chest feel tight.

*No.* She wouldn't let that happen. She had always fought for the people she cared about. She was never going to stop fighting for Flynn and Ruby.

Even at six months old, Ruby already seemed to have a great sense of self, which in large part was due to Flynn's deep love for her. Whereas from what Cassie could glean from the little Flynn had said about his upbringing, no one had ever shown him the love he deserved.

Well, she sure as heck was going to show him now.

When she drove up to her cabin, she found Flynn and Ruby standing on the front steps, the little girl waving. Just that quickly, Cassie's fears, worries, and nerves started to fade. They didn't completely go away—she'd need to stay on her toes with Flynn. But she wouldn't have him any other way than as exactly who he was.

After parking, she walked up to the pair and immediately took Ruby into her arms to cuddle her tight and kiss her cheek. Not intending to leave Flynn out, she shifted Ruby to one hip, put one hand on his face, then went on her tippy-toes and pressed a kiss to his cheek too.

His skin was warm beneath her touch, and he smelled delicious, like clean male and forest. One innocent kiss, and she was already heating up from head to toe.

It took her far longer than it should have to realize something was different about her cabin. "Those are new flower boxes!" She turned back to Flynn. "Did you do this for me?"

"Rory helped."

Though she was surprised to hear that the two men had worked together on the project, she was certain without being told that it had been Flynn's idea. She'd never wanted to kiss him on the lips more than she did right now, but she'd promised him that she'd leave that kind of kissing on the back burner for the time being.

"I love them." She moved close again to press her lips against his cheek. "Thank you."

She could have sworn the slow brush of his cheek over hers, and the way he seemed to want to keep her close for as long as possible before she drew back, was no accident.

"Ruby helped me load up her backpack with diapers, a bottle, a snack, and an extra change of clothes, just in case she needs it." Though he was talking about the baby, his voice was slightly hoarse. As though he was having to fight just as hard not to kiss her. "I hope we didn't forget anything."

Ruby responded by shoving the stuffed elephant at Cassie. She laughed, saying, "Don't worry, of course we're taking your bestie with us."

Cassie pretended that the elephant was whispering into Ruby's ear. *"I can't wait to go on a hike with you today, Ruby! We are going to see the most amazing things while we're together. And there's no one that I'd rather be with than you."*

With that, Cassie had the elephant kiss Ruby's cheek. When the baby giggled, she made it kiss her other cheek. Then her belly, and both her hands and feet too. Each kiss made her laugh harder. Even Flynn was laughing by the time Cassie was through.

Since Ruby's car seat was already installed in Flynn's rental, they piled into his car.

"How have things been going since I saw you yesterday?" she asked. It had been barely twenty-four hours, and yet it felt like she'd been away from Flynn and Ruby for much longer.

"I took Ruby down to the water, and she loved splashing in the shallows. After that, we came back home, ate some dinner, and read *Wheels on the Bus* until she fell asleep."

"Sounds like the perfect afternoon and evening."

He took his eyes off the road for a split second to look at her. "Almost perfect. She kept wanting me to make Ellie the elephant talk, but I can't quite figure out how to get the voice right. I nearly called you to ask."

She grinned, beyond pleased that they'd missed her last night, the same way she'd been missing them. "You could have called me. Now that I'm here, we can practice doing the voice together, if you'd like."

"Actually, speaking of Ellie the elephant—" His expression turned serious. "—I've started a new screenplay."

"That's fantastic news." Picking up on the enthusiasm in Cassie's voice, Ruby started clapping from the backseat. "But what does Ruby's stuffed elephant have to do with it?"

"The elephant is in the story."

"Wow." Cassie couldn't contain her surprise. "I didn't see that coming."

"Neither did I. If this new project ever sees the light of day, I'm going to give you co-writing credit."

"I don't need credit for anything. Although I am curious—how have you managed to fit a stuffed elephant with polka dots into a thriller?"

"It's not a thriller. I'm not sure *what* it is just yet, only that Ellie the elephant has a fairly major role."

"Double wow."

"I know Smith and Valentina are expecting a thriller. The thing is…" It seemed as though he couldn't find the words to express what he was feeling.

"You want to keep going with what you've started, don't you? If for no other reason than to see where you end up."

"That's exactly it." He sounded more than a little surprised by her insight.

She indicated he should turn right at the four-way stop, then said, "Sometimes, if I'm not working on commission, I'll just start building with random pieces of candy. Only to find out partway through that they weren't so random after all, that I needed to express something I was feeling or trying to figure out. Remind me once we stop the car, I have pictures on my phone of some of the wild and weird things I've made. Things that I always think won't move anyone but me, but that end up touching other people in ways I hadn't imagined they would."

The driving directions got a little more complicated after that, so for the rest of the ride, she focused on getting them to the trailhead. Once they parked, she was about to get out of the car when he stopped her with a hand on her arm.

"The pictures of your wild and weird confections," he reminded her. "I'd like to see them."

She pulled her phone out of her pocket and scrolled through her photo album. "Here's one. I had just seen something in the news that really upset me. I wanted to make something that would help me find my way back to beauty. To hope. To love. A woman in Colorado now has it hanging on her living room wall."

The candy structure in the picture was two feet tall and two feet wide and utilized candies in every color. Some parts were straight, some were curvy, some were dark, but most were light.

"Amazing." He looked up from the photo. "You've created modern art out of candy. And just like the heart you entered in the contest, you've created *emotion*."

"If you keep saying such nice things, you're going to give me a big head."

"You could never have a big head. Though if anyone deserves one, it's you."

"I just make things out of candy. It's not a big d—"

His mouth was on hers before she could get the rest of her sentence out.

Their second kiss was as breathtaking as the first. This time, however, she didn't make herself pull away. Instead, she happily kissed him right back.

"You're right," he said when they finally drew apart. "That's the perfect way to get you to stop putting yourself down."

The kiss had scattered her brain so much that she couldn't quite follow. "What was I saying that you objected to?"

"That your confections aren't a big deal." He brushed the pad of his thumb over her lower lip, making her shiver with desire. "They are, Cassie."

For a moment, she thought he might kiss her again. But then he said, "I swore to myself that I would leave our kiss on the back burner, like we agreed."

"I'm glad we didn't." Right then, Ruby let out a little shriek from the backseat. "Uh oh, I don't think someone likes being left out of the conversation for this long."

They got out of the car, then unstrapped Ruby— and Ellie the elephant, whom she was clutching to her chest—from her car seat and transferred them both to the backpack on Flynn's back.

Cassie was beyond glad that Flynn had kissed her. She was less thrilled, however, by how conflicted he was over it. What would it take for him not only to trust her, but to understand that she trusted him, regardless of his secret past?

As they took the short walk from the parking area to the edge of the pond, she hoped the magic of exquisite nature all around them would help. The sky was a perfect blue sprinkled with fluffy white clouds, the trees were so green it almost seemed unreal, the water was like a mirror reflecting all the beauty back to itself, and the smell from the trees and shrubs and wild-blooming flowers was absolutely divine.

"Jordan Pond is one of my favorite places." She was proud to be able to share this spot with Flynn and Ruby, to show them one of the many reasons she loved Maine and Mount Desert Island.

"I can see why." Even Ruby seemed awed by the view of the pond and the mountains and trees that surrounded it. "I had no idea Maine was like this. Every day, I feel luckier that Smith suggested Ruby and I come here."

"I feel lucky too." She reached for his hand, feeling even luckier when he threaded his fingers through hers and held on tight. It was amazing how much comfort—and sensuality—there was in being palm-to-palm with him.

"Why don't we walk a bit," she suggested, "and then when we get to a little cove up ahead, Ruby can have her snack and play by the shore."

"I doubt we're going to be able to keep her out of the water."

"Then we can become wet, muddy messes together." Cassie blew a kiss to Ruby, who was making nonsense sounds from the backpack and swinging her elephant around in the air to make it dance. Turning back to Flynn as they walked along the waterline, she asked, "Do you have more research questions for me?"

"I've never spent time with a big family like yours. I'd love to know more about what it's like. Particularly about how it seems to work so well when there are so many people with different personalities and goals."

"My guess is that it's down to my parents for always being there for us. Which isn't to say that they let any of us walk all over them—or each other, for that matter. They didn't put up with much when we were kids. Still don't."

"I can see your father being strict. But your mother is always so friendly and full of smiles."

"My father's actually the softie, whereas my mother rules with an iron whisk."

Flynn raised an eyebrow. "I don't think your father has any intention of being soft with me."

"No." There was no point in acting like that wasn't the case. "He clearly wants to put you through the wringer. I have faith you'll win him over, the same way you've clearly won Rory over. Hudson and Brandon too, once you finally meet them."

"Great." He shook his head. "Two more brothers who will be angling to tear me limb from limb when they find out I'm kissing their beloved sister."

She wasn't sure he realized that he was talking about the two of them in future tense, rather than as though they'd exhausted their limit of only two kisses. His brain might be telling him he couldn't be with her...but his heart was clearly already on board.

She grinned. "You'll like Brandon and Hudson. In fact, you've probably already stayed in at least one of Brandon's hotels, somewhere in the world. He's the owner of the SLVN hotel brand."

Flynn looked impressed. "Is there anything your family can't do?"

"Random Sullivan fact: We're terrible at playing soccer. Anyway, Brandon is pretty much always on a plane getting ready to open a hotel in another far-flung, exotic destination. And Hudson lives in Boston with his wife."

"I'm surprised only one of you is married, considering that your parents are such great role models for wedded bliss."

"Don't be fooled—they yell plenty. Especially Mom. She calls it *letting off steam*. But actually, the fact that they have such a great relationship is probably part of the reason why most of us haven't rushed to jump into anything serious. Their love story is a lot to live up to."

"Funny," he said, "I always thought only people who had parents with bad marriages were prone to holding off on their own. I hadn't realized it could be just as hard to live up to a great relationship. Although your brother's marriage must be good if he was willing to take the plunge."

She frowned. "I hope Hudson and his wife are in a good place. I'm not sure they are, though. My sister-in-law doesn't come to many family events anymore. We've always been so open with each other, but these past few years, Hudson is more and more closed off. It's hard feeling like I'm not really a part of his life anymore. I just hope that if he's ever ready to talk, he knows I'll always be there for him."

"He knows it, Cassie. I can promise you that."

"Same goes for you. If you ever want to talk." She held out her arms. "I'm here." Not wanting to push too hard, she gestured to the cove. "And here we are, at the beach I mentioned earlier." She reached up to take Ruby out of the backpack. "Are you ready for your snack, little miss?"

Cassie loved holding Ruby on her lap while she fed her Flynn's homemade pea puree. Ruby happily wolfed it down—splattering only a little bit onto the three of them this time—then pointed toward the water.

"Time to swim!" Cassie took off Ruby's shoes and socks, then rolled up her leggings, before doing the same for herself. She looked at Flynn, who was still fully dressed. "You're coming in too, aren't you? It won't be nearly as much fun without you."

But he was staring at her toes and didn't answer.

Though Cassie wasn't particularly wild in her clothing choices, she liked to splash out in secret sometimes. Case in point—her toenails were painted a particularly seductive shade of red, which she had matched to her bra and panty set.

"I've never thought feet were sexy before." Flynn's voice sounded a little hoarse.

She was surprised by how shy she felt when he'd already seen her nearly naked in her workshop. But that was before their kisses. Before she'd ever imagined that he could desire her.

Ruby, who had thought they were just about to get into the water, made a slightly grumpy sound, so Cassie swung her up into her arms, calling out to Flynn, "Last one in is a rotten egg!"

Holding Ruby around her chest, she lowered the baby's feet into the water. Ruby immediately started splashing and giggling as they got wet.

Soon, Flynn was there too, his cuffs rolled up so that Cassie could see he had surprisingly sexy feet too.

Then again, everything about him was sexy. If he ever let his walls fall enough for them to go to bed together, she could imagine just how mouthwatering the rest of him would be…

Her cheeks were flushed as she said, "You're right, Ruby really loves the water. Good thing you brought her a full change of clothes."

"Looks like you're going to need one too."

She hadn't planned on going into the pond when she'd dressed for their hike today. Now she realized that Ruby's splashing had drenched not only the baby, but her white T-shirt too, so that Flynn could quite easily see just how well her nail polish matched her red bra.

"When we get back to the cabin," he said, "you can change into something of mine while I make dinner. That is, if you're free tonight."

She lifted her gaze to his, knowing he wouldn't have made that offer lightly when he was such an intensely private man. "I am. I'd love to have dinner with you and Ruby."

Ruby reached for Flynn, then, and it was such a joy to watch him play with his little girl. He might not have much experience with babies, but that didn't stop him from instinctively understanding exactly what she needed—someone who wasn't afraid to plop down in the water with her and splash around with total abandon. And when Ruby surprised herself by flinging water in her own face and started to cry, he soothed her so sweetly that Cassie's insides turned to complete mush.

"We're coming up on Ruby's nap time," he said a while later, when all three of them were pretty much soaked. "I'll just get her into dry clothes, and then we can head back."

A few minutes later, Ruby was nodding off as she rode in the backpack. Not wanting to wake the baby, neither of them spoke. But this time, Flynn was the one to reach for Cassie's hand.

Their kisses might still be on the back burner, but right now, Cassie was more than happy for the simple pleasure of Flynn's hand over hers.

# CHAPTER FIFTEEN

From the first moment he'd set eyes on Cassie, Flynn had warned himself over and over to leave her alone. Smith hadn't sent him to Maine to seduce his cousin— and Flynn knew he had no business messing around with a forever kind of girl.

But he hadn't counted on how incredibly seductive her smiles were. Or how impressive she was, on every level. Or how much fun she was to be around.

And especially not how sweet her kisses tasted.

Tonight she was looking particularly adorable wearing one of his T-shirts and a pair of his sweatpants while her wet clothes tumbled in the dryer. She was reading Ruby's favorite book to his little girl, and maybe he should have been sick of hearing about the bus wheels going 'round and 'round by now, but when Cassie was singing along with the story, he found himself as captivated as Ruby, who was bouncing on her lap.

He was so busy staring at the two of them—and marveling at how different this night was from any he'd ever had in Los Angeles—that he almost forgot to stir the stir-fry he was making for dinner.

Flynn hadn't cooked for many people over the years, but whenever he had, they were always surprised by how well he knew his way around the kitchen. That's what came from taking care of both himself and his sister while they were growing up. If he hadn't made dinner, more often than not, Flynn and Sarah would have gone hungry. As an adult, he'd found cooking to be the perfect activity when he wanted to think through plot holes in his screenplays.

"That smells so great," Cassie said, while Ruby happily played with the pull-tabs in her book. "Mom is going to be so impressed when she finds out you can cook."

"Don't get your hopes up too high," he warned. "My food won't be a patch on your mom's."

"I wish I were closer so that I could kiss you again to stop you from saying that." She shot him a warning look of her own. "You'd better stop talking trash about yourself, or I won't be responsible for my actions."

Flynn had never been more tempted to talk some serious trash about himself, if only to see what Cassie would do with her mouth, and maybe her hands, to shut him up.

At the same time, when he could think beyond how much he wanted her, he had to wonder if she had a point. He wasn't a kid cowering in the corner any-more—so why did he always talk about himself as though he were?

Of course, it was easier to focus on getting dinner on the table, so he shoved the question to the back of his brain. "If you could get Ruby set up in her high chair, I'll bring our plates over in a couple of minutes."

"Hear that, little miss?" Cassie said to Ruby. "It's dinnertime. Yum yum!"

Cassie looked so natural as she stood with the baby on one hip, brought her over to the high chair, and strapped her in, that Flynn's chest clenched tight with emotion.

"I almost forgot," she said. "I brought Ruby a new bib." From her bag, she took out a bib printed with elephants. "These are some of Ellie's relatives," she said to Ruby, who happily traced her little fingers over the fabric. Cassie looked over at Flynn. "I apologize in advance for all the elephant paraphernalia I'm bound to give her from here on out."

He knew she was teasing. And yet instead of teasing back, he was perfectly serious as he told her, "You never have to apologize for anything, Cassie."

"Same goes for you, you know."

But he did. Because he still hadn't told her the truth when, more than anyone, she deserved it from him.

He brought over a selection of purees for Ruby,

then put plates of rice and Thai-style stir-fry in front of Cassie and himself. "I can take over feeding Ruby," he said, but she waved away his offer.

"You know I love taking care of her." The words were barely out of Cassie's mouth when Ruby nailed her straight between the eyes with a spoonful of pea mash. Laughing, she added, "Even if it means getting a pea-flavored skin and hair mask." She wiped off her face with one finger, then licked it. "Mmmm. That's really good."

Flynn hoped she wasn't waiting for him to say something in response, because just watching that one small act had lit a major fire inside of him.

He'd never wanted anyone so badly. Never craved a woman's taste this much. Never endlessly fantasized about stroking someone's soft skin. Never had to stop himself from spinning one wicked scenario after another about the two of them inside his brain.

He shoved a forkful of food into his mouth, but didn't really taste it. At this point, he just needed to get through dinner without dragging Cassie against him and ravaging her mouth.

And any other part of her he could reach.

"*Oh, Flynn.*" Judging by the rapturous sounds, Cassie was enjoying her meal. "You're a brilliant cook." She closed her eyes on another mouthful, and he let himself drink her in for a few precious seconds.

"You've *got* to make this for my mom. Thai flavors are something she's always wanted to master, but never gets quite right." She put down her own fork to help Ruby eat a few more bites. "Where did you learn to cook like this?"

"I spent some time in Thailand a few years back, doing some research for a movie. One of the street food vendors let me cook with him for a few days."

"No wonder you're such an amazing storyteller. When you do something, you really give it your all, don't you?"

The way she looked at him with stars in her eyes made him uncomfortable when he hadn't done a damn thing to deserve her admiration.

She held up a hand. "And be careful how you respond to that, or you risk my mouth on yours again."

Yet again, he was tempted to say absolutely anything at all that would convince her to kiss him. Instead, he told her, "Research is one of my favorite parts of the job. Especially when I have the privilege of trying on someone else's life for a little while."

Though it was obvious she wanted to ask his reasons for wanting to shed his own life for someone else's, she simply smiled and said, "I really need to get over being such a wimp so that I can see your movies."

"No." He felt strongly about this. "I don't want you to watch them."

"Why not?" She frowned, clearly unable to understand his reaction. "Everyone says how amazing they are."

His gut was churning now. "I was a different person when I wrote those movies. I hope I've become a better man since Ruby came into my life." *And you too, Cassie. Since you've shown me just how beautiful honesty and hope can be.* "I don't want her watching my movies either, when she gets older."

Cassie put her hand over his. Ruby, who was sitting between them, mimicked her, her little hand touching his. "I won't watch them if you don't want me to. But even if I did, I already know who you are."

"Cassie…"

He put down his fork. He had to tell her the truth, had to explain that she *couldn't* know who he was, because no one did. Even if it meant she never looked at him like that again. With admiration and—even more important—her heart in her eyes.

But Flynn had no idea how to start. How to say the words he'd sworn he would never speak to anyone. How to strip away the man he'd created out of thin air to expose the boy he'd wanted to forget ever existed.

Ruby let out a yell that yanked him from the battle he was fighting inside his head. She was rattling her high chair, obviously no longer thrilled about being strapped into it.

"Would it be okay if I let her out of her high chair?" Cassie asked. "She could sit on my lap while we eat, if that would make her happier."

Grateful to Ruby for the reprieve, however short, from having to confess both his lies and his painful truths, he said, "Actually, once she's done eating, she tends to be happiest on the rug with her toys."

Cassie wiped down Ruby's face and hands, took off her bib, then put her down on the floor nearby with her mobile blanket and zoo of stuffed animals. Flynn knew that buying her anything that caught her eye in the local toy store was a bad habit, but he wanted to do whatever he could to make up for the first five months of her life, when he hadn't been there to watch over her.

Only, Ruby didn't seem interested in her toys tonight. Instead, as soon as Cassie sat down at the table again, Ruby reached out for her, obviously wanting to be held by one of her favorite people.

Cassie was about to go pick her up when Flynn saw Ruby's expression change into something that looked like determination. Somehow he knew to put his hand over Cassie's to keep her in her seat.

A few beats later, Ruby leaned forward onto her hands, then hoisted her bottom up into the air. She stayed like that for a few moments, almost as though she couldn't believe what she could do with her limbs.

*"Flynn,"* Cassie whispered. "Is she…?"

Before Cassie could get her question out, Ruby lifted one foot and then one hand and moved herself forward. After a beat, she did the same with her other foot and hand. When she fell over, she lay on her back and wailed.

Flynn and Cassie flew to her side. "You crawled!" he said at the same time that Cassie exclaimed, "She crawled!"

He lifted Ruby up high and kissed her cheek while Cassie leaned forward to kiss her other cheek. That was when he realized there were tears in Cassie's eyes.

"You just blew my mind, little miss." Cassie's voice was thick with emotion. "Do you want to do it again?"

Flynn wanted to cherish this moment forever, one in which he was filled with so much love and pride that there was no room for darkness. But he knew Cassie was right, that he should put Ruby down so that she could crawl again.

"I love you, Ruby." He kissed her again, then set her down.

Ruby frowned, and he thought she might cry again as she reached for Cassie.

"Cassie," he said quickly, "last time she was trying to get to you. Maybe if you move a few feet away, that will convince her to do it again."

Cassie scooted to the edge of the rug, and as Ruby

watched her get farther away instead of closer, Flynn could pinpoint the exact moment the determined look came back into her eyes. Ruby wanted so badly to get to the woman she adored, she'd do whatever it took.

Rocking forward onto her hands again, she popped her bottom into the air. The next thing he knew, she was motoring across the floor like a baby-shaped spider.

Cassie cheered Ruby on as she held out her arms for the little girl to crawl into. "Ruby, you're amazing!"

Ruby giggled when Cassie popped a kiss onto her lips, then squirmed to get down and do it again.

Flynn marveled in awestruck silence as she spider-crawled all over the living room and kitchen.

"Looks like it's officially time to babyproof." Cassie's voice was full of love as she moved a basket of kindling off the floor by the fireplace and onto the counter.

How had things already changed so fast? One moment, Ruby was happy sitting in one place playing with her toys, and the next she was exploring every nook and cranny. He'd barely started to get his head around the way things were, only to realize that he would have to come up to speed yet again.

For the next half hour, Ruby was in constant motion—and so were Flynn and Cassie as they pulled anything at all dangerous out of her reach. Thankfully,

Cassie had already put in electric socket safety covers before they moved in, so by the time Ruby wore herself out and crawled into Cassie's arms for good, the living room and kitchen were well babyproofed.

Flynn made up a bottle for Ruby, which Cassie gave to her. Normally, he gave Ruby a bath before bed, but tonight she was so tired from crawling that he simply cleaned her tooth and gums, then changed her into a new diaper and pajamas. After he laid Ruby down in her crib, Cassie tucked Ellie the elephant into the crook of her arm, then covered her with a blanket. After giving her good-night kisses, the two of them tiptoed out of the room and closed the door. The baby monitor he kept with him would alert them if Ruby woke up and needed anything.

Tonight, with Cassie and Ruby, he'd learned how good it would be to have a happy family of his own. But now that Ruby was asleep, his temporary reprieve was over.

It was time to tell Cassie the full, unabridged truth.

# CHAPTER SIXTEEN

"Ask me, Cassie." They had only just returned to the living room. Flynn had avoided this moment his entire adult life. But he'd never be able to look himself in the mirror again if he avoided it with Cassie. "I've told a million lies in my life, but I can't lie to you anymore. Ask me the three questions I asked you, and I'll tell you the truth."

She held out her hands to him, the same way she'd reached for Ruby a short while ago. And just like the baby, he grasped them like a lifeline.

"Before I ask you anything, there's something you should know." She moved closer, close enough that when she went up onto her toes, her lips were nearly against his. "I love you." She pressed a finger to his lips to forestall any protests. "And don't you dare say I haven't known you long enough to fall in love. I don't need any more time than this to know what's in my heart. And that it's only ever beat this way for you."

If hearing her say she *loved* him hadn't already been enough to steal his breath away, her mouth against his would have done it.

Her kiss echoed the three little words as passion wound like a velvet ribbon around them.

When she finally drew back, she lifted her hand to his cheek. "And now I can't wait to hear all about you, Flynn. Your secrets, your edges and dark places—even if none of them have ever succeeded in covering up the light inside you, no matter what you think."

Desperation clawed at him to take everything she offered. The absolution, the promise of a happy future with her pure sunshine smile lighting up every moment.

But he knew how insidious that hope could be...especially when he'd done nothing at all during the past twenty years to earn it. Until Ruby came into his life, he'd lived only for himself.

Forcing himself to let go of her hands and step away, he made himself answer the first question, though she hadn't yet asked it. "My world turned upside down pretty much from the beginning."

She frowned, but didn't reach for him again as he went to stand by the window. Night in the forest should have been pitch black, but Cassie—being Cassie—had hung a metal sculpture in the shape of a heart on a nearby tree. It was strung with little white lights so that when darkness fell, the heart was illuminated.

In the reflection of the window, he saw her slowly move to the couch and sit.

"My parents should never have been parents," he said. "I came nine months after they got together. My sister was born fifteen months after me. Fortunately, we were the only two kids they had. Your parents had the ultimate meet-cute romance, something straight out of a rom-com movie. Whereas my dad met my mom because he was her dealer."

Flynn made himself turn to face Cassie, certain he'd see shock on her face from his revelation. Instead, she simply looked like she wanted to wrap him in a big hug.

He would have given *anything* for that hug. But he'd only just started spilling his guts, and if he stopped, he wasn't sure he'd be able to start again. Not when every word he spoke felt like it was covered in spikes.

"He was a nasty drunk, and she was weak enough to think she loved him. Loved him in a way she never loved me or Sarah. We were only ever in his way, and we learned to hide in corners or behind closed doors. I did everything I could to protect my sister, but—" His throat closed as he thought of all the days, the nights, he hadn't been able to keep his sister out of harm's way by taking her place. "I was a small kid and didn't fill out until much later, so I couldn't keep her safe."

*"Flynn."*

He was momentarily paralyzed as he watched Cassie cross the room to him. But then he remembered. One touch would break him. And then, given the force of his need—and his desperation to know a truly loving touch for once in his life—he might break *her*.

He made himself take a step back, hoping she'd understand his clear cue.

*Stay away for your own good.*

By the time she stopped barely a foot from him, his chest was heaving as though he'd just sprinted down the long driveway.

"I left when I was seventeen," he ground out. "Dropped out of high school and headed for Los Angeles on a Greyhound bus. From everything I had read and seen on TV, Hollywood was as different from the middle-of-nowhere town I grew up in as I could find. I came up with my new persona on that bus. *Flynn* from Errol Flynn. *Stewart* from James Stewart. My real name is—"

He couldn't manage the words, not just yet. But Cassie waited until he was ready.

"Joe." He let out a long breath. "Joe Miller."

He saw a droplet of water fall to the floor in front of him before he realized a tear had slid down his cheek. A tear for that kid who had been so damn scared of everything that his greatest accomplishment had been deleting himself from the world.

The next thing he knew, Cassie's arms were around him. She was stroking his hair, his back, and pressing kisses to his cheeks in the same way she so often kissed Ruby.

For all that he'd told himself she'd leave once she knew the truth, now that he was finally being honest...he'd known better. Known she would only come closer. That she would hold on to him and not let go.

But having her arms around him scared him even more than her leaving would have. Because now that he knew how good it felt to have Cassie to hold, he also knew how horribly empty his life would be without her in it.

Had that fear not been eating away inside of him, he might have given in and wrapped his arms around her too. Instead, he made himself stand stiff and still. Made himself grind his teeth to keep from begging her not to leave.

She brushed away his tears with her fingertips. "Something tells me I would have loved Joe Miller just as much as I love Flynn Stewart." Her smile was as warm and real as her heart. A heart that was so big she had found room even for him.

"You shouldn't love either of us."

"Don't you dare tell me how to feel about you, Flynn." It was a relief that she hadn't called him Joe.

He could never be that boy again, not even for her. "You loved your sister, just as you love Ruby."

"I did love her, but I let her down. She died because I didn't fight hard enough for her."

"That's not true." She was fierce in her defense of him.

"It is. I should have moved heaven and earth to keep her from falling into the same dead end of drink and drugs and abusive relationships as our parents. I should have stopped at nothing to get her out, to get her away from that world and everyone in it. I shouldn't have let her turn down my help again and again and again over the years. But in the end, I only saved myself. I left her behind to overdose in some dirty room. Dying like our dad, who ended up OD'ing in prison after he killed someone in a drug deal. Dying like our mom, who drank herself to death. If I had known Sarah was pregnant, I would have made her leave with me, no matter how much she needed the drugs or whatever guy she thought she couldn't live without."

Now that he'd started to tell the truth, he had to get the rest out, had to come completely clean.

"I've been lying to everyone since I was seventeen. Lying about where I grew up, lying about who I am, lying about where I went to school, lying about my parents dying in a car crash. I even created fake social media pages to back up my stories so that no one could catch me out. And all the while, I convinced myself it was the only way I could start over, start fresh, to keep from being dragged down by my family history of drugs, booze, and death. I told myself I wasn't hurting anyone by becoming someone new. Until I met you." He nearly reached for her then, before remembering that he didn't deserve to touch her. Didn't deserve to have her in his arms. "Until I lied to you. And I felt like the lowest of the low."

After a few moments, she asked, "Is that everything you need to tell me, Flynn?"

*God no.* There was so much more he needed her to know.

That she was the best person he'd ever known.

That she'd brought more joy into his life than he'd ever thought to have—and into Ruby's life too.

That he'd started falling for her the first time she smiled at Ruby.

And that she wasn't the only one who had fallen in love. He'd barely made it to that first night, when she'd come to take care of Ruby, and him too, before he'd fallen for her.

She was still waiting for his response. "I need to tell you what I'm afraid of," he said.

It was the second question on the list that always defined his work. For once in his life—for Cassie—he was going to face up to the hard truths rather than hiding behind fictional characters.

"I'm afraid of *this*." His heart was pounding so hard as he spoke, he could feel the pulse points throbbing in his neck, his wrists. "I'm afraid of finding someone like you...and knowing you won't stay, because you deserve so much more. So much better."

"Why don't you think you can conquer that fear, Flynn?" Cassie not only wasn't leaving, she also wasn't afraid to ask him question three. "What makes you think you're not good enough, tough enough, determined enough, to be not only everything I deserve, but everything *you* deserve too?" Before he could respond, she moved close again and put her arms around his neck. "Especially when I've known all along that you already are."

Before he could respond, her mouth was on his, and he was lost in the sweet passion—and the unconditional love—of her kiss.

# CHAPTER SEVENTEEN

Cassie poured every ounce of the love she felt for Flynn into their kiss.

Pain throbbed just beneath the surface of her skin for all that he'd suffered. For all the guilt he carried inside. For the shame he hadn't been able to shed as easily as his real name and childhood history.

She wouldn't hide how deeply she hurt on his behalf in the future. But tonight, what he needed wasn't a reminder of darkness. He needed light. He needed joy.

And if all those layers of pain, of shame, of guilt, made it impossible tonight for him not only to hear, but to fully believe her when she said *I love you*, then she would say it to him another way. With her lips on his, and her hands caressing his skin, and her body pressed against his.

All her worries that she wasn't enough for him, that she wasn't as pretty as his model girlfriends, now seemed utterly pointless. It was long past time for both of them to know that they were *more* than enough, not only for each other, but within themselves too.

Her brother and sisters had said she didn't give herself enough credit. It turned out they were right.

She wouldn't make that mistake again.

And she wasn't going to let Flynn do it anymore either.

Deeply certain of how good they were going to be together, even if their road to forever might be riddled with bumps, she smiled against his lips. He must have felt it, because he drew back.

"You make me smile," she told him. And soon, she hoped to see him smiling again too. "You also make me feel like I'm wearing *way* too many clothes."

Holding his gaze, she bunched the bottom of his T-shirt that she was wearing in her hands, then pulled it over her head and tossed it aside. Soon, his sweatpants were lying in a pile at her feet. Leaving her wearing only her sexy bra and panty set that matched her nail color.

Though he simply stood and stared, she knew without a doubt how much he wanted her from the way his eyes had gone dark. From the way he clenched his hands at his sides. And from his heart pounding against her open palm, hard and fast, when she laid her hand on the center of his chest.

"Anything you want," she said softly, "I want too." She wouldn't force anything on him, though. Wouldn't take away any of his personal power, when so much had already been taken from him. "But if you don't want to make love to me, I won't—"

"*I do.*" He covered her hand with his, barely leashed power radiating from his touch. "I've never wanted anything more than I want to make love to you. But I would never forgive myself if I hurt you."

"You would never hurt me." It was as much a fundamental truth as the fact that he would never do anything to hurt Ruby.

"You deserve a gentle lover. And I want you too much to be gentle."

Her lips turned up again as she closed the distance between them, pressing the length of her body against his. "I don't want gentle. I want *you.*"

★ ★ ★

Flynn had never thought he'd be so close to heaven...or that getting there would put him on the precipice of hell.

Because as she stood, so radiant, in front of him, how could he do anything but reach for her...and tear the red silk and lace clean off her gorgeous skin?

He didn't realize what he'd done until he looked down and saw the fabric in his hands. Only the sound of her laughter stopped him from begging for her forgiveness.

"I knew sex with you would be *amazing.*"

He could barely wrap his head around the fact that his sweet candymaker actually liked it when he tore off her clothes. Just as he could hardly believe the vision of beauty before him.

"You're the one who's amazing." His words were hushed. "You're just as beautiful as I dreamed you'd be."

Her curves were beyond luscious, her skin the prettiest peaches and cream. There was no way he could have stopped himself from dropping the fabric to the floor and reaching for her soft skin.

He curled his hands around her hips to pull her against him, then lowered his mouth to hers for a lingering kiss. Savoring, relishing the sounds of pleasure she made as he stroked his tongue over hers, the way she moaned softly when he nipped lightly at her lower lip.

He might not be able to give her the perfect forever she dreamed of, no matter her faith in him, but at the very least, he could give her pleasure. Breathlessly intense bliss that he vowed would be beyond anything she'd ever known before.

Lifting her into his arms, he kissed her as he carried her to the couch. He waited until the very last second to lift his lips from hers as he lowered her to the leather, then knelt on the rug between her thighs.

"I want to taste every inch of you." He pressed his

mouth to the crook of her neck. "I want to find out what makes you moan. What makes you gasp. What makes you cry out with pleasure." He nipped at her ear before adding, "What makes you come apart."

"*Yes.* I want all of that too."

Again and again, it blew his mind that the most wonderful woman in the world—not to mention the sexiest—could want him.

He threaded his hands into her hair and kissed her again, knowing he'd never get enough of her sweet mouth. Slowly, he ran kisses along her jawline, down the sensitive skin of her neck, then over the curve of her shoulder. Feeling her shiver as he dipped his tongue into the hollow of her collarbone, he did it again, loving the way she tightened her grip around his waist as she instinctively pulled him in tighter between her legs.

Her skin was impossibly soft as he stroked, as he caressed, as he worshipped her curves, her hollows, her peaks, her valleys. She arched into his touch without fear or reservation—and with a smile. The smile that had captivated him from the first.

A smile that turned into a gasp as he curved his hands around her full breasts.

She wasn't the only one losing her breath as he cupped the soft flesh, then slid his thumbs over the taut peaks. Lowering his mouth to one breast, he feathered his breath over one aroused tip, then licked out against her.

A low moan came from her throat as her hands slid into his hair. *"Flynn."*

Giving her pleasure was the greatest pleasure he'd ever known. Miles beyond anything he'd ever experienced before. He couldn't begin to imagine how good it would be when she climaxed.

Just thinking of it had him tightening his lips over her. In response, she pulled him closer to the heat of her body. Every taste he had of her only made him want more—and made him more desperate to give her the ultimate pleasure.

Control spiraled away as he cupped her breasts and feasted on her. Her moans gave way to cries of pleasure, and from the way she was rocking her hips against him, he knew he wasn't the only one who needed more.

His heart nearly pounded out of his chest in anticipation of *more.* In anticipation of slick heat and even louder cries of ecstasy.

Forcing himself to go slowly, he ran kisses down from her breasts, over her stomach and hips. "So beautiful," he murmured against her flushed skin.

She kept her curves mostly hidden beneath loose-fitting clothes and aprons, and though he wanted her to celebrate her beauty, to be totally honest he was glad that there were few other people who knew her the way he did. Cassie was a sexy, hourglass goddess. One who outshone every Hollywood star, every supermodel.

With his mouth barely above her sex, he gripped her hips and lifted her to him. The first taste nearly broke him. By the second, he was completely lost in her, his self-control destroyed.

He couldn't remember to be gentle as he thrust with his tongue, again and again, deeper and faster, until the first tremors started to run through her.

In a flash, he replaced his mouth with his hand as he moved over her on the couch. He needed to see her face when he brought her over the edge. Needed to know for sure that *he* had finally brought *her* some joy.

Her eyes had been closed, her head thrown back, as she undulated against him. But as she reached for him to thread her fingers into his hair, she opened her eyes and stared into his.

*"I love you,"* she whispered, then brought his mouth down to hers. And as she unabashedly gave him every ounce of her pleasure, the smile on her lips as she kissed him made him smile too.

# CHAPTER EIGHTEEN

Cassie had never felt so good in all her life.

Flynn was so much bigger that she couldn't quite take in a full breath as he lay pressed against her. And yet, she never wanted to unwrap her legs or arms from around him.

He smelled absolutely divine too. The most delicious man alive.

Following her instincts—from here on out, she wasn't going to hold anything back—she licked his neck. His skin tasted salty, and so yummy that she did it again.

He lifted his head, his eyes dark as he looked down at her. "You're so beautiful."

No one had ever made her feel so cherished. Like she had been made to be worshipped. As though she was utterly special. Perfect, even.

She smiled at him, full of the sweetest joy. "You took the words out of my mouth." She stroked her fingers across his jaw. "And I can't *wait* to give you the same pleasure you just gave me."

He put his hand over hers, stilling it. "Tonight is for you. For your pleasure. All I want is to make you happy."

"You do," she said softly. "But you're wrong about one thing. Tonight isn't just for me. It's for *both* of us."

"Cassie, you don't have to—"

She stilled his protest with a kiss. "Nothing we're doing here goes just one way. For everything I give you, you're giving me just as much." She pressed her lips to his again before he could argue with her. "And right now," she said when they finally came up for air, "I want you to give me yourself."

His eyes darkened even further. But, fortunately, not from shadows this time. "Tonight, I'll give you absolutely anything you want."

Though she wasn't crazy about his *tonight* qualifier, she recognized how much it had taken for him to say even that. Small steps—that's what would get them there in the end, and she would celebrate every single one of them with the man she loved.

But first, she needed to make one big move, shimmying out from beneath him so that he was now lying under her on the couch.

He looked stunned at how quickly she'd flipped their positions. "How did you do that? I'm so much bigger than you."

"A girl has to learn some pretty tricky moves when

she's got four brothers. Although I never thought those moves would come in handy at a moment like this."

At the mention of her brothers, Flynn's jaw tightened. "They're going to kill me. Not just your brothers, but your fath—"

"No." She kissed him to soften the harsh word. "Tonight is about you and me." To further reinforce her words, she reached for the buttons on the long-sleeved shirt he'd changed into after their hike. "And *me* wants *you* naked."

She loved seeing his lips curve up at the corners at her bashing of the English language in the name of lust.

Her hands were steady as she undid the buttons on his shirt. Until she had it nearly open, that was. *"Oh God."* He was *too* beautiful. She'd thought she was prepared to see him without clothes on, but clearly, if his bare chest and washboard abs were anything to go by, she most certainly was *not* ready.

"Cassie?" Fear leaped into his eyes with lightning speed, his muscles going taut beneath her. "What's wrong?"

"Nothing is wrong." She kissed his lips, his cheeks, his forehead, his chin, until she felt his tension ease. "You're *ridiculously* good-looking. I'm a little…" She searched for the right word, fanning herself with her hand as she finally settled on, "Overcome."

He surprised her by laughing. A small sound of joy,

but one she deeply relished. "You always know how to make me laugh," he told her. "Even now, when I can't keep my hands or mouth off you."

But when she pulled his shirt all the way open and laid her hands over the bare skin of his tanned, well-muscled chest, their smiles fell away.

"Mine." She'd never thought she was a possessive person—until tonight, when she couldn't deny the truth. She lifted her gaze to his. "You're *mine*."

"*Yours.*"

He hadn't echoed her words of love. Hadn't come anywhere close to that specific, traditional sentiment. Yet with one word—*yours*—he'd not only stripped her heart bare, he'd also given her his heart, whether he was ready to admit it to himself or not.

"I am yours," she whispered. "Tonight and always."

With her heart laid completely on the line, she decided it would be wisest to steal any potential protests by lowering her lips to his skin and kissing her way across his chest.

She closed her eyes to drink in every sensation of their lovemaking—the scent of arousal, the heat they generated, the feel of his slightly rough hands over her sensitive skin, the taste of him on her tongue.

*More.* She wanted so much more.

While he ran his extremely talented hands over her

breasts, she knew her fingers wouldn't obey her brain for much longer under his sensual onslaught. She undid his belt, then popped open the button of his jeans, unzipped him, and stripped the rest of his clothes away.

Again, when she looked down his body, she lost her breath.

As a candymaker, Cassie had never been renowned for her self-control when it came to enjoying her creations. But it wasn't until tonight with Flynn that she realized that her lack of control extended to lovemaking.

Greedy, she reached down to cover his hard, thick length. On a lusty sigh of pleasure, she curled her fingers around him and slowly stroked. His hips seemed to lift into her hand of their own volition, and her lips found their way to his shaft in the same way. Unable to deny the desire ripping through her, head to toe, one soft kiss became another and another, until she couldn't wait to take every last gorgeous inch into her mouth.

She was so lost in pleasure that she was stunned to find herself sitting astride Flynn a moment later. "No fair," she protested. "I wanted—"

This time, he was the one swallowing her words with his kiss. "I love the way you touch me." She saw the truth of it in his eyes. "But I can't wait another second for you, Cassie. For *all* of you."

The fierce need in his voice—threaded with the same desperation she felt for him—was nearly enough to take her over the edge of pleasure again. Helped along, of course, by the sinful slide of his erection against her bare sex.

She closed her eyes and tilted her head back as she rocked over him, both of them soon slick with her arousal. Then he threaded his hands into her hair and drew her mouth back down to his.

Their kiss was wild, irresistible, reckless. So reckless that she was lifting her hips to take him inside without any thought for the consequences, when he stilled her with firm hands on her hips.

"Cassie." He nipped at her lips. "We need protection."

For a long moment, she couldn't process his words. Finally, they sank in. "I have some. In my bedroom. I mean, your bedroom."

But oh, how she hated to leave this perfection behind, even for long enough to run out of the room to grab a condom.

As though he didn't want to be separated either, he stood and carried her into the bedroom. "Don't let go," he whispered into her ear.

"Never," she whispered back, wrapping her arms and legs tighter around him.

He grabbed the monitor, the baby still softly snoring in her crib, then headed down the hall into the bedroom. Flynn laid her on the bed, then climbed over her, the muscles in his arms, his abs, his thighs and glutes rippling.

"Please tell me protection is nearby." He spoke the words around the kisses he was raining up her bare legs, then her stomach and breasts, and finally her mouth. "Because I'm not going to have the self-control to stop us again."

"In the bedside table." At least, she hoped a condom was in there. Certain that there weren't going to be any men in her near future, she'd done a cleanout a while back. She wasn't the world's best cleaner, however, so if luck was on their side—

He held one up, triumphant as he tore it open and put it on. She wrapped her arms around his neck, and he slid his hands beneath her hips. His eyes held hers, and though she'd already told him in a dozen different ways how much she wanted to be with him, she knew instinctively he needed to hear it one more time.

*"Love me, Flynn."*

The words had barely left her lips when he moved into her, perfect pleasure taking her over as her body welcomed his heat, his strength, his innate sweetness. The smile she gave him came from the very center of her heart, the deepest part of her soul.

"My beautiful Cassie."

Oh yes, she was *his* in every possible way as he moved his hands from her hips to thread his fingers with hers and hold them tightly beside her head.

Together, they began to move. Slow and sweet, then fast and just the right side of rough.

If she could have, she would have held on to the precious moment forever. But pleasure this strong, this meant to be, couldn't be denied.

Higher and higher she went, flying freer than she'd ever known she could, all because Flynn was soaring with her. Higher and higher until pleasure exploded inside her, a euphoria unlike anything she'd ever known.

And as Flynn followed her into bliss, she knew no moment had ever been as right as this one in the arms of the man she loved.

# CHAPTER NINETEEN

Cassie woke to the sound of Ruby playing in her crib. Flynn was holding her tightly against his chest as though even in sleep he'd been afraid she might leave him alone.

She pressed a kiss to his chest, which she had been using as a pillow, then slowly slid out from beneath his arm. When he began to stir, she whispered in his ear, "Sleep. I'm going to get Ruby."

From the way his eyes closed at her reassurance, it was obvious that he needed the rest. And just as she had been thrilled to be a part of Ruby's bedtime ritual, she was excited about getting to see the baby first thing this morning.

Cassie put on the flannel shirt hanging on the back of the chair in the corner, then walked across the hall into Ruby's room. "Good morning, little miss!"

Ruby pulled herself to standing in the crib and gave Cassie a huge smile. Of course, Cassie had to give the baby kisses galore as she lifted her out of the crib, making both of them giggle.

"Let's get you into a new diaper and outfit, then we'll make up a yummy breakfast bottle and join your very handsome daddy."

Fifteen minutes later, with Ruby happily guzzling her first bottle of the day, they headed back into the master bedroom. Cassie climbed into bed with the baby in her lap, propping pillows behind her back so that they could sit together comfortably.

She'd only just gotten settled when Flynn opened his eyes. She smiled at him. "Good morning, sunshine."

He blinked at her and Ruby, obviously trying to make sense of what he was seeing while still in the fog of sleep. A short while later, he came fully awake and moved to sit beside them, his chest bare, the sheet and comforter around his waist.

"I didn't hear her wake up." He was clearly berating himself for it as he gently caressed Ruby's cheek with the back of his hand.

"She was singing in her crib. I let you know that I had her so that you could go back to sleep."

Cassie had to work to push away the hurt that he hadn't reached out to her yet. She'd known this was likely how he would behave in the morning, hadn't she? As though she were now off-limits again, even though they'd been so intimate the night before.

She vowed not to give up, no matter how difficult it might be to convince Flynn that he was everything she'd ever dreamed of in a partner.

"I thought it would be nice to bring Ruby into bed with us."

"It is nice," he agreed, his deep voice still a little hoarse from sleep. Or maybe it was that she hadn't fully buttoned his shirt when she put it on, and his gaze had dropped to the curve of her breast revealed in the open placket.

Last night, when they'd made love, it had been obvious that he thought it was one night only. Not because he didn't want more time with her, but because he thought he didn't deserve more. She wouldn't shy away from dealing with it, even if the sparks that were certain to fly meant the end of their relaxing morning together in bed.

"Do you want to talk about last night and where we go from here?" she asked. "Or do you need coffee before we dive into it?"

He ran a hand over the stubble on his jaw. "You don't hide from anything, do you? Even just to sweep things under the rug for a couple of hours?"

Ruby finished her bottle, and as she shifted the baby to burp her, Cassie said, "I figure after everything we shared, there isn't any point in hiding things. So how about we start with the easy stuff? Like how *great* last night was." When he didn't say anything—or make any move to touch her—she reached for his hand. "But it was about more than just phenomenal sex. I feel so close to you, Flynn. Closer than I've ever felt to anyone else. And I love every second of being in your arms."

He was silent for a long moment, but when he lifted her hand to his lips and kissed it, that one small hint of emotion sent relief moving through her.

"Last night with you..." He looked into her eyes. "It wasn't just sex for me either. Every moment with you is one I will cherish forever. No one but you has ever accepted me for who I really am. But—"

Ah, here was the part she had known was coming.

"I'm still not good enough for you."

She hated having to raise her voice. But he was really starting to piss her off, especially after she'd already made it clear what she thought of his negative self-talk. "You don't respect my judgment when I say I think you're a good man? When I make it perfectly obvious that I want to be with you and Ruby? When I tell you I love you?"

"Of course I respect your judgment. But what if your judgment is clouded when it comes to me?"

"Why would it be clouded? Do you think I'm deluded by how much I like looking at you? By how much I like kissing you? By how much I like what you do to me in bed?" She let one loaded question after another fall, before gentling her voice. "Or do you think I'm making excuses for you because I feel sorry for what you've been through?" When he didn't reply, she growled, "Because if that's what you're thinking, then you've *never* been more wrong."

With that, she kissed Ruby, then handed the baby to him. As always, he scanned Ruby's face to make sure she was happy, then cradled her close. The little girl let out a contented sigh as she snuggled against the chest of the person she loved most in the world.

"I wish you had known love as a child, Flynn," Cassie told him, her heart laid as bare as her body. "The same love you're giving to Ruby right now. The same love I knew when I was growing up. But even without it, your heart is so big, so strong, so true, that I'm constantly astounded by you."

"Can't you see that I'm just trying to do the right thing for once in my life?" he replied. "I don't want to tell you any more lies, which is exactly what I would be doing if I said I thought this could work out between us, when what I really need to do is get the hell out of your life so that you can be with someone who is worthy of you."

*"The right thing? Worthy?"* She really was fuming now. "I'm very happy to hear that you're not going to lie to me anymore. Because, no matter what, I would never lie to you. And I'm no longer going to hold back either. Which is why I'm going to tell you that you're being a stubborn jerk." She let the words land. "If you

would open up your eyes, you'd see what I see in you. But you're so busy beating yourself up all the time, so busy replaying the story of the life that you wrote for yourself in Los Angeles, that you're not giving the real you—or us—a chance."

Her words were fierce enough that even Ruby's eyes popped open.

"Sorry, sweet girl," Cassie said as she stroked the baby's hair back from her face. "I don't normally yell, I promise." She turned back to Flynn and, in a more reasonably pitched voice, said, "In case you think my yelling means I'm not in love with you anymore, think again. I'm still head over heels for you. And I'm not going anywhere—even if you try your darnedest to push me away."

She put her hands on either side of his face and kissed him. Then she did the same with the baby, before gently placing Ruby back in Flynn's arms and heading out of the bedroom to get her clothes out of the dryer. On the threshold, she realized she needed to say one more thing.

"I'm going to head in to work now, but don't you dare take this discussion, and my obvious frustration, as an excuse to disappear on me. Even if you don't think you can trust yourself not to hurt me, I'm telling you right now that I trust you not to do the only thing that truly would hurt me. Because now that I've finally found the two people I'm convinced I'm supposed to be with for the rest of my life, I'm not going to lose you both. And no matter what it takes, I'm going to convince you too."

* * *

No one had ever fought for Flynn. He'd always had to face difficult situations entirely on his own. Or worse, pretend everything was fine, no matter the pain, the fear.

But Cassie wasn't afraid of *anything*. She hadn't held back from confronting him and telling him exactly what she felt and needed.

One day, he hoped Ruby would be like her. Strong. Unafraid. And so full of love it would constantly amaze him.

He had so much to learn from Cassie. And now that he knew what it was like to bask in her love, he only craved it, craved her, more. And yet...

There still was no denying that she deserved better.

He could hear Cassie opening and closing the dryer and got up off the bed with Ruby to go beg her for forgiveness. Not only for being a stubborn jerk, but for being too selfish to stop himself from taking her to bed. He wanted her to understand that it would kill him to walk away from her—but how could he do anything else when he'd never forgive himself if any part of his past, present, or future hurt her?

Unfortunately, Ruby was suddenly badly in need of a diaper change. And by the time he had cleaned her up, Cassie was gone.

The cabin felt empty without her. Even Ruby looked sad.

"You're not the only one in love with her." He couldn't say the words to Cassie, not when it would only make it harder to let her go, but he couldn't hold them in another second. "I love her too, Ruby. More than she'll ever know."

Obviously able to sense how much he needed comfort, Ruby held up Ellie the elephant and rubbed the stuffed animal against his cheek.

"Thank you, sweetheart. You know just how to cheer me up, don't you?"

She confirmed it by giving him a kiss.

Of everything he'd done in his life, he wasn't sure how any of it could have been good enough to deserve not only Ruby, but these life-changing days in Maine with a woman who had revived the heart he had thought was forever dead.

# CHAPTER TWENTY

Cassie hadn't looked at her phone since yesterday's hike. When she got into her car and finally thought to pull it out of her bag and check it, she found a half-dozen texts from her sisters. First, asking if she wanted to meet for a drink after work. Then, when she didn't answer, asking if she was with Flynn. And this morning, another round of texts insisting that she *tell them everything* and that they'd be waiting to have breakfast together in Lola's studio.

She sent a quick text saying she would be there in half an hour, then put her phone back into her bag and got on her way.

She didn't blame her sisters for wanting the details. If she were in their shoes, she would expect the same. The three of them had had their arguments over the years, but they also had each other's backs, no matter what. There was nothing Cassie couldn't say to her sisters.

It was what she wanted from Flynn—for him to know that he could trust her with absolutely everything.

*Was that too much to ask?*

All she knew was that after spending a night in his arms—and after experiencing such sweet pleasure that she was still reeling—she wanted to feel that close to him always.

But how could they ever get there if he couldn't trust her?

And, more important, trust himself.

In her apartment, she took a quick shower, then threw on jeans and a tank top. Bang on thirty minutes, she walked into Lola's studio, where she could hear her sisters chatting.

"Your coffee delivery is here." She handed Lola and Ashley the to-go cups, then walked over to admire the new fabric designs her sister had pinned up around the room. "These are gorgeous. This magenta one is practically glowing."

"That's *your* glow you're seeing reflecting back at you." Lola scanned Cassie from head to toe. "Well, well, well. I haven't seen you look this satisfied in…pretty much ever."

Ashley was also regarding her with a laser focus. "Did you stay the night with Flynn?"

Cassie couldn't hold back her smile. For all that her relationship with Flynn was nowhere near settled, she was still incredibly happy.

"I did."

"And…?"

She hadn't held back with Flynn this morning, and she wasn't going to hold back with her sisters either. "I'm in love with him. And Ruby too."

Lola and Ashley shared a look.

"Go ahead," Cassie said. "Whatever the two of you are thinking, spit it out."

"First," Ashley said, "I think it's great that you and Flynn had a hot night together. After all these sex-free years I've been having, I can definitely see the upside of a night with a guy who knows what he's doing. Which, from your glow, he clearly does. But…" She looked at Lola again, who nodded for her to continue. "We also want to make sure that you're not so busy swooping in with your Superwoman cape to take care of Flynn and Ruby that you forget to take care of yourself."

"I'm not." When her sisters both raised their eyebrows at her quick denial, Cassie said, "I'm not going to deny that they've brought out the nurturer in me." She tried to figure out the best way to explain what she was feeling. "But it's so much more than that. Ruby is a ball of joy, so of course I love spending time with her. And Flynn—no one has ever seen me the way he does. I'm not talking about my looks, although he does seem to like them quite a bit, which is lovely. But *me*. Just as I want to understand what makes him tick, he wants to know all the same things about me. And when I'm with him…" She smiled again. "I've never been so happy. Or felt so absolutely certain that I'm in exactly the right place, with exactly the person I'm meant to be with. You were trying to get us together from the beginning, Lola, and whatever instinct possessed you to do that, you were right. It might have taken me a little while to come around to the truth, but now I'm one hundred percent certain that he's the one for me."

"Wow." Lola looked more than a little shell-shocked. "And here I thought you were just going to tell us about your night of hot sex. You really *are* in love with him, aren't you?"

Cassie nodded. "And he's in love with me too."

"Did he say that?" Ashley asked, her eyes huge.

"No." Cassie plopped down on Lola's comfy couch. "He's too busy saying he's not good enough for me to get those other three words out."

"Wait a second," Lola said, holding up her hand before Cassie could say more. "I want to make sure I have everything straight. After a week of will-we-won't-we, the two of you finally got it on last night, at which point you told Flynn that you're in love with him, and he said—"

"I should wait for a much 'better' guy to come riding in on his white horse for me."

"I take it he thinks his viewpoint is warranted?"

Ashley asked.

"His story isn't mine to tell," Cassie said. "But yes, he's convinced that his past has to define his future. He's wrong, though. And I was hoping you two might have the magic answers so I can get him to see it."

Lola held up her hands. "If you're looking for me to possess some sort of love potion, you're talking to the wrong girl. The best you're going to get out of me is a killer dress for your awards ceremony this weekend. Which," she said as she unzipped it from its hanger, "is ready for your final fitting."

When Cassie turned to Ashley for input, her sister said, "You know I'm not exactly Little Miss Sunshine when it comes to matters of the heart. And the truth is that I think I understand some of what Flynn is feeling. Because once you've screwed up badly enough, you're never quite convinced that you won't mess up again just as badly."

Cassie hated that Ashley was still beating herself up over getting pregnant in high school. "What would it take to convince you to risk your heart again, Ash?"

"The guy would have to be great with Kevin."

"Obviously," Cassie said. "But what about *you*? How would he have to treat you? What would he have to do to break down your walls and make you look at everything in a new light?"

"I'm going to need a few minutes to think that one

through," Ashley said, "so you might as well go put on the dress."

Cassie went into Lola's changing area, quickly shed her jeans and shirt, then shimmied into the formfitting dress. Slipping on the heels Lola had thoughtfully sourced for her to wear with it, she tied her hair into a knot in an updo and walked back out.

Both of her sisters whistled. "Damn, you really are *gorgeous* in my dress." Lola whipped out her phone and started taking pictures before Cassie could stop her. In any case, she was far more interested in hearing what Ashley had to say.

"Have you come up with an answer yet, Ash?" Cassie asked.

"I'd have to know that the person I was risking my heart for loved me no matter what." Ashley's expression was as serious as Cassie had even seen it. "And even if I *did* screw up because I was scared, or if I tried to push him away—and I'm thinking both of those things are pretty much a given considering my emotional battle scars at this point—he'd have to prove to me that he wasn't going anywhere. That he had faith in me, and in us, to weather anything that came our way."

"So you're not asking for much, then?" Lola teased.

Ashley huffed out a laugh. "I'm certainly not holding my breath that Mr. Perfect is going to show up anytime soon—on a white horse, or otherwise." She shot Cassie a rueful look. "Sorry I'm not more help."

"Actually, you've been a huge help. Both of you."

"How?" Lola asked.

"Well, Ashley has confirmed that I was right to tell Flynn this morning that I'm not going to give up on him, no matter what." She grimaced slightly. "I kind of yelled it at him, actually."

"You?" Ashley's eyebrows went up. "Yelling?"

"He was being utterly infuriating and stubborn."

"I swear, this is getting more interesting by the second," Lola murmured. "In any case, you were getting to how I've helped...?"

"You've given me the dress of a lifetime. So even if Flynn believes the right thing to do is keep his distance from me, I'm fully confident that your dress will make him lose control again. If I can convince Flynn to go with me to Portland for the awards ceremony, will you guys help Mom watch Ruby? I know he came to Maine with Ruby for the chance to be anonymous, but maybe if he knows he has our support, he'll consider trying to live a normal life where he doesn't have to wear glasses and baseball caps and sit in corners every time he goes out."

"I'd love to help," Ashley said. "And Kevin will be thrilled to get to spend more time with her."

"As long as I don't have to change diapers," Lola said, "I'm in too. In fact, I've been mulling over creating some fabric for a girls' line. Ruby would be the perfect model."

"Great. I'll text Mom to make sure she's free too, in case Flynn says yes. Now I just need to figure out a way to get him on board with my plan." Cassie looked down at her dress. "Maybe I should wear this when I ask him, in case I need to seduce him into going to the ceremony with me."

"I know I've teased you more than once about making more of your sex appeal," Lola said, "but you've always led with your heart. Regardless of how great your night was in the sack with Flynn, it's your huge heart that he's fallen for. And it's that same big heart that is going to make him realize that he doesn't have to beat himself up anymore over his past, because you're always going to be there to love him." .

"I agree one million percent," Ashley said. "You've got one of the biggest hearts of anyone I've ever known. Flynn would have to be a fool to throw that away…even if there's a little yelling, here or there," she added with a teasing glint in her eyes.

"But just in case there do need to be some sexy hijinks along the way to convince Flynn to see sense—" Lola went over to one of her cabinets, pulled out a couple of condoms, and gave them to Cassie. "Now you're ready for *anything*."

Cassie eyes were wet as she hugged her sisters. "I love you guys."

# CHAPTER TWENTY-ONE

Flynn was sure that Beth Sullivan would see the truth of what he'd done with her daughter when he dropped Ruby off at her house. But Cassie's mother was all smiles and obviously overjoyed to see Ruby again.

Soon, he was in the library, his laptop open. Only today, instead of staring at the blank screen, he couldn't get the words down fast enough.

> *The ten-year-old boy is wearing a dirty shirt and pants. He's sitting alone on the playground of his elementary school, a rough place full of bullies who've learned everything they know from their even rougher parents.*
>
> *He's deep inside his head, making up stories of other worlds, of anywhere but here, when he sees her. A pretty little girl with a wide smile, walking onto the playground. She doesn't seem to notice the bullies—and certainly doesn't seem to be afraid of them—as she heads for him.*
>
> *"Hi. I'm Cassie. I'm new here. What's your name?"*

*The boy blinks at her as though she's speaking a foreign language, before answering. "Joe." His voice sounds funny, like he isn't used to talking much.*

*"Want to play, Joe?"*

*Too stunned to do anything else, Joe follows her over to the swings he never uses.*

*Cassie, already swinging, asks, "What's your favorite color?"*

*Joe is still sitting on the swing with his feet flat on the ground as he replies, "I don't have one." It's a lie—he loves the color green, but he doesn't want her to make fun of him like everyone else does. He's pretty sure ten-year-old boys aren't supposed to still have favorite colors.*

*Cassie smiles at him, seemingly not bothered by his response as she hops off her swing to push him on his. "Mine is pink and purple polka dots."*

*Joe is stunned by how strong she is as she sends him soaring on the swing. It's been so long since he's felt like he's flying, like he's free. "That's not a color."*

*"I know. It's lots of colors, which is even better! Do you want to know a secret?"*

*Of course he does. But he's afraid she'll make him tell her his secrets, so he shakes his head.*

*She doesn't let that stop her. "My elephant is the one with all those colors."*

*Joe turns to look at her from the swing. "You*

*have an elephant?"*

*"Want to come home with me today to meet her? Because she told me she wants to meet you."*

*He can't figure out how Cassie could possibly have an elephant, let alone one who talks. But even if he could, he hasn't been to anyone's house in a long time and doesn't have any friends anymore. Not since things have gotten even worse at his house. He can't see why someone like Cassie would want to have anything to do with him. And if the other kids think she's his friend, they'll treat her badly too. He needs to say no, if only to save her from potential harm.*

*But just as he's about to shake his head again, he hears the sound of her laughter. That's when he realizes that she has hopped onto her swing and is soon flying just as high in the sky as he is.*

*Her laughter is what finally pulls the truth from him. "Yes. I want to come home with you. And meet your elephant."*

Flynn's fingers stilled on his keyboard. He'd never felt like that while working on a screenplay before—like he was simply taking dictation.

And it wasn't until he read through what he'd just written that he realized what he'd named the protagonist of his story.

Joe.

It was tempting to change the name, to back away from the truth like he always had before. But he'd told Cassie today he was done lying to her, and he knew deep inside himself that it wasn't enough to stop lying only to her. He needed the courage to tell the truth to everyone from this point forward. He owed it not only to Cassie, but to Ruby.

One day, Ruby was going to be a ten-year-old on schoolyard swings, and it was his job to teach her how to be honest and friendly when she got there, rather than withdrawn and wary, the way he'd been. More than anything, he wanted Ruby to know joy.

He'd asked Cassie to teach it to him so that he could pass that knowledge on to his little girl. But when he'd finally let Cassie's joy take him over completely for one perfect night, come morning he had immediately pushed her away.

Not that she'd let him push her far. On the contrary, she'd said she wasn't going to let him disappear on her. That she wanted to spend the rest of her life with him and Ruby.

He rubbed his hand over the tightness in his chest as he thought about the apology he owed her. Not only for the way he'd behaved today—but also because he couldn't shake his fear that if he dared give his heart to her, he'd only end up hurting them both in the end.

One thing was certain, at the very least: He

couldn't write another word until Cassie knew how sorry he was and that none of his behavior was her fault.

Having left his car at her mother's house, Flynn practically sprinted the three blocks from the library to Cassie's workshop.

He hadn't even made it two hours without needing to be with her. How the hell was he going to go back to the opposite coast? Especially when he knew Ruby would miss her just as much.

He rang the bell, and when Cassie opened the door to her workshop, she looked so beautiful that there was only one thing he could think to do, only one possible option left, no matter how many times he told himself he couldn't have her.

Flynn kissed Cassie the way he wanted to kiss her every time she laughed and made his heart dance inside his chest.

He kissed her the way he wanted to kiss her whenever she was playing with Ruby and giving his little girl the love he'd never known himself.

He kissed her the way he wished he could tell her he loved her too.

When he finally lifted his mouth from hers, her skin was flushed and her eyes bright. The next thing he knew, she was pulling him inside, locking the door behind them, then jumping into his arms in the hallway.

She was so damned sweet as she wrapped her legs around his hips. He craved everything about her. Her luscious lips beneath his. The little gasps she gave when he lightly bit one of her earlobes. How tender, how wonderfully sensitive, the skin was along her neck as he ran his tongue down it.

*"Flynn."*

He loved the way she said his name. Like she was already on the edge of coming apart for him.

Desperate to feel her pleasure, and to give her the same joy she'd always given him, he was unbuttoning and unzipping her jeans when he realized he didn't have any protection with him.

Because he'd promised himself he wouldn't touch her again.

"Don't stop," she urged him, putting her hand over his and sliding it lower.

*Holy hell.* She was so hot, so wet, so ready for him. And when she kissed him like that, her tongue dancing with his, her teeth nipping wickedly at his lower lip, he was nearly lost again. But he couldn't hurt her, would never forgive himself if he did.

"I don't have any protection." He barely managed to get the words out when all he wanted to do was keep kissing her. And to love her with everything he was.

"I do." She reached around to her back pocket and pulled out shiny foil packets. "Not just one, but two!"

She looked so triumphant that he had to kiss her again. And give silent thanks that, inexplicably, she had two condoms in her pocket.

Together, they worked to strip off her clothes before tearing off his. Soon, she was ripping open the first packet.

"I wanted to be the one to put this on you last night," she said in a husky voice, nearly stealing what was left of his control by sliding it on him. "I'm glad I didn't have to wait long for my turn." When she was done, she lifted her eyes back to his. "I can't wait to love you again."

"I can't wait either."

She put her hands around his neck and re-wrapped her legs around his waist. "Then don't."

Before she could take her next breath, he was inside of her. She arched her breasts into his waiting mouth, where he laved first one, then the other. Soon, her breasts were flushed and damp from both his tongue and the light scrape of his teeth over her beautiful skin.

Somewhere in the back of his head, he knew he should be gentler with her, that she couldn't be used to someone like him, someone from the wrong side of town who had never learned how to be soft or gentle.

Only to realize that *he* was the one working to keep up with *her*. And when she begged him to take her harder, faster, higher, how could he do anything but give her everything she wanted?

Making Cassie happy was the only thing that mattered. And even if he still wasn't convinced that he could make her happy for the rest of her life, at least when they were both naked and in each other's arms, he had no doubts.

When her climax finally took them both over, her laughter as she clung to him had him smiling against the top of her head.

And wishing that he could bottle this feeling and hold it forever.

# CHAPTER TWENTY-TWO

"I came to say I'm sorry for being a jerk—a stubborn one—this morning."

Cassie lifted her face from the crook of Flynn's neck. He smelled so good and felt even better as he held her so tightly. As though he never wanted to let go of her.

She smiled as she looked down at their naked bodies. "Apology accepted."

His surprised laughter sounded like heaven. Only Ruby's laughter was as beautiful, and as precious, to Cassie.

"This wasn't how I planned on saying it." His expression grew serious as he brushed the hair back from her face. "I—" He stopped himself. "Maybe we should put our clothes on so that I'm not so tempted to put that second condom to use."

She would happily have stayed naked with him and used that second condom, but it was obvious that he had something important to say.

Reluctantly, she unwrapped her legs from around

his waist. But though her feet were on the ground again, she still felt as though she were flying.

That was what being with Flynn did to her—he lifted her up higher than anyone, or anything, ever had.

How she wished she could do the same for him…

Minutes later, they were fully clothed and sitting on the stools in her workshop with cups of freshly brewed tea. Flynn hadn't said anything while she'd been heating up the water and getting out the tea bags. She'd remained silent to let him get his thoughts together.

Now, he took both of her hands in his and said, "I never expected to meet anyone like you. Especially not after becoming a father in the blink of an eye. I'm not telling you this to make excuses for my behavior. You deserve so much better than the way I acted this morning after we woke up. But I need you to know that whatever I do, it's not because you're anything less than perfect. It's not because I don't want to be with you. It's not because I don't…" His grip tightened on her hands as he cut himself off. "I care about you, Cassie. So damned much. And to hear that you want to be with me and Ruby—I honestly can't believe it. I wish…" He lifted her hands to his lips and pressed kisses to them. "I wish I could make you promises. I wish I could be the man you deserve. But up until four weeks ago, when Ruby came into my life, I was nothing more than a selfish shell of a man."

She couldn't stay quiet anymore. "You weren't. And don't say that I didn't know you back then, so my opinion doesn't count. Because no matter how many times you've said that your past was worthless, I know it can't be true. People don't change from bad to good in four weeks. You've always been good, Flynn. Just as you've always had so much love inside you."

"I want to live up to the man you think you see," he said in a voice made raw with emotion. "I just don't know if I can."

"I do." She leaned forward to kiss him softly. "Every time I see you with Ruby, you prove it to me. Which isn't to say that I'm expecting you to be perfect either. You're not the only one feeling your way forward here. Heck, *I'm* the one who was yelling this morning. Even Ruby was stunned."

"Your version of yelling and everyone else's are drastically different. Trust me, I have plenty of experience with yelling, and you most definitely weren't."

She leaned her forehead against his. "I wish you didn't have so much experience with that. I wish I could have been there to protect you when you were a child. It's taking everything inside of me to accept that I can't go back and change the past." She prayed he would let himself hear her when she added, "You can't change the past either, Flynn. No matter how much you want to."

"I dream about my sister," he told her in a low voice. "Every night since she died, I've dreamed that she's taken my hand and has finally agreed to leave it all behind—the drugs, the drink, the abuse. But every time, she slips away and I can't get her back. Until she's gone, just another statistic. And my heart is broken." His chest shook as he inhaled a ragged breath. "Last night was the first night I didn't have the nightmare. Because you were there."

"See?" She drew back so that she could look into his eyes. "We're already helping each other."

"You're helping me. I can't see how I'm helping you."

"You really can't?" She couldn't stop her voice from rising again. "Do you think I always glow like this?" She held out her arms so that he could get a good look at her. "Do you think I'm always this inspired?" She gestured to the half-built candy art piece on her worktable that was coming together faster, and better, than anything she'd ever made. "Do you think I haven't been longing for someone to look at me the way you do, to really see *me* and absolutely love what he sees? Do you think that when I'm with you and Ruby, I'm not happier than I've ever been before? That I'm not more in love than I even knew was possible?"

It wasn't until she heard her voice echoing off the

walls that she realized how loud it had become. "I'm sorry, I'm doing it again. Yelling when what I really want to do is make everything better for you."

Thankfully, Flynn didn't seem to mind, because he was pulling her back into his arms. "It still doesn't count as yelling, you know." He lowered his mouth to hers, and when he was only a breath away, he said, "And you *do* make everything better. Every single second we're together—and even when we're not—you're changing everything for the better."

Though he'd said he couldn't make her any promises, his kiss said differently. She didn't need to hear three little words fall from his lips to know that he had promised her his heart.

They were halfway to needing that second condom when the front door buzzed. Cassie was breathless as she lifted her mouth from Flynn's. "I'm expecting a delivery."

They were both trying to right each other's hair and clothes when the visitor stepped into her workshop.

"Cassie, honey…what the hell?"

*Oh God.* It wasn't a delivery after all.

Though it was impossible to hide the evidence that they were together, Flynn jumped away from her. "Mr. Sullivan, sir." He looked like he was on the verge of saluting, or bowing, or something else equally ridiculous, given that neither of them had anything to apologize for.

"Hi, Dad." Cassie gave her father a kiss on the cheek. "This is a nice surprise. I didn't know you were going to come by today."

Ethan Sullivan was so busy glowering at Flynn that it didn't look like he was going to respond anytime soon. At which point Cassie decided, *In for a penny, in for a pound.* Her father was going to have to get over this ridiculous wariness with Flynn. Otherwise, the two of them were going to have some serious words. And he'd better watch out, because she had been working on her yelling.

Deliberately, she went to Flynn's side and slid her hand into his. She didn't want her dad to feel she was choosing sides, but she needed him to understand that she was serious about Flynn—and that she wouldn't let anyone hurt the man she loved.

Flynn was stiff as a board beside her, obviously waiting for her father to rip their hands apart. And probably lock her in an ivory tower while he was at it.

But he didn't pull away. Another spark of happiness lit inside of her. Instead, he stood by her side the same way she was standing by his.

"Was there something you wanted to talk with me about, Dad?"

"I came to wish you luck this weekend."

She smiled. "Thank you."

"And to give you this for good luck." He handed her a locket with a four-leaf clover inside.

"Oh, this is lovely." She let go of Flynn's hand to hug her father. And whispered into his ear, "You don't have to worry about me. Flynn is a good man, just like you."

Her father's arms tightened around her before he let her go, then headed out the door without another word. She was about to go after him when Flynn beat her to it.

"Your father and I need to have a talk." A beat later, he was gone.

She was tempted to follow him, but she'd lived with four brothers long enough to know that neither Flynn nor her dad would thank her for getting in the middle of what they needed to work out.

Good thing she trusted them both enough to know that even if things got worse before they got better, neither of them would wound the other out of anything but concern for her.

They were two of the most hardheaded men she'd ever met.

It was no wonder she loved them both so much.

★ ★ ★

"Mr. Sullivan!"

One moment, Flynn had been vowing to stay away from Cassie, the next he'd been making love with her against the wall, and now he was chasing her father down the street to beg for his permission to be with her.

He had no doubt that Ethan was going to say no. Why would he do anything else?

Nonetheless, Flynn knew he couldn't fail this first huge test. It was long past time to buck up and fight for something that really mattered.

Even if he came out battered and bruised on the other side, Cassie was worth fighting *any* battle for.

Deep in his heart, Flynn had known it from the moment he'd first seen her smile and reach for Ruby so sweetly.

"Please," he called when the other man didn't slow his pace. "I need to speak with you about Cassie."

At last, her father stopped in his tracks. He didn't turn around right away, and Flynn got the sense he was girding himself for battle. When Ethan finally turned, Flynn knew by the glint in his eyes that he'd been right: Ethan Sullivan was hell-bent on fighting for his daughter's heart.

That made two of them.

"My family has opened up our homes to you. My wife is at this very moment watching your little girl, and *this* is how you repay us? By dragging Cassie into a sordid fling?"

Flynn had to work to keep his voice even. "With all due respect, nothing Cassie and I have done is sordid." On the contrary, every moment with her had been made of wonder and awe, at least on his part. "I understand that you're furious with me, but don't take it out on your daughter, or let me come between the two of you, when she has done nothing whatsoever to deserve your scorn."

"You're damned right she hasn't done anything wrong." Her father's glare was as hot as a thousand suns. "And I'd never turn my back on her. Even if you're intent on dragging her into your mess. I knew the first time I set eyes on you—"

"That I'm not good enough for her." Flynn had no problem whatsoever finishing Ethan's sentence. "You're one hundred percent right. I'm nowhere near good enough. I agree wholeheartedly that she deserves the best man in the world to stand by her side and support her through thick and thin, better or worse, good times and bad. And if I were you, I would want me out of the picture too. But..."

Jesus, was he really about to say this to her father? Lay out his deepest wishes and insecurities, so that the other man could shred them to pieces?

"Everything she thinks I am," Flynn said in a voice made strong by love, "everything she thinks I can be, everything she sees when she looks at me—I want to be all those things. I want to be the man she deserves. I want to give her everything she's ever dreamed of and more."

Ethan stared at him in silence before finally responding. "There's one hell of a big difference between wanting to do something and actually sticking to your goal when times get tough and giving up is easier. I'm not at all surprised that you care for my daughter. You'd be a fool not to. But you haven't told me one damned thing about what you're planning to do to prove to all of us that you're worthy of her."

Flynn's back was entirely against the wall. Deservedly so. But he wasn't angry with her father for pointing out his deficiencies. On the contrary, he respected Ethan Sullivan more than ever. One day, if he needed to confront one of Ruby's boyfriends, he was going to remember this moment, when he'd learned what a *real* father did to keep his children safe.

"I may never be able to prove it." Flynn's voice was low, but determination thrummed in every word. "But you have my guarantee that I'm done backing down. I'm done running. And I'm done lying. Not only to Cassie, but to you and your family." He looked her father square in the eye and laid himself bare for the second time in his life. "My real name isn't Flynn Stewart. It's Joe Miller. I'm from a dead-end town in

Illinois. I left when I was seventeen and have told a thousand lies to erase my past and get the things I felt I was owed as reparation for my childhood, for growing up as the kid of violent addicts. I tried to get my sister out, but I wasn't strong enough, wasn't determined enough, to convince her to leave behind the only life she knew. By the time she died and I learned about Ruby, I hadn't spoken to Sarah in over a year." He felt drained dry by his confession, but he wasn't done yet. "I've vowed to give Ruby everything I couldn't give my sister. Not just money and opportunity, but love. The same soul-deep, boundless love I feel for your daughter. The same love I still can't believe she feels for me. And even though I know everything I just told you only proves what a bad bet I am for Cassie, I'm still going to ask you to give our relationship a chance."

"And if I say no?"

"Then I'll be back tomorrow to ask again. And the day after that. Until you see that when it comes to your daughter, not even her terrifying father is enough to make me run again."

Flynn had spent his whole adult life putting words together. Which was how he knew there was nothing more to be said today, nothing he could do to convince Ethan Sullivan to give him a chance. But by tomorrow, he'd make damn sure he had another argument ready. As many as it took.

"So you're not going back to Los Angeles?"

"Ruby loves it here, and so do I." Ruby was going to do so well growing up in this tight-knit community rather than in one of the overcrowded, often dangerous schools in Los Angeles. "You're stuck with me in Bar Harbor for the duration."

"I see." Flynn couldn't read Ethan's expression. "In that case, let me make one thing clear to you: While I'm sorry that you've had a tough life, if you use your past as an excuse to hurt so much as one single hair on my daughter's head, and if you treat her with anything other than the deepest love and respect, I will personally tear you limb from limb."

"If I hurt her, I would do it for you, sir."

"I'm happy to hear we're in perfect agreement." With that, Ethan reached out, gave Flynn's hand a quick shake, then turned to walk away. He'd gone only a few feet when he turned back. "Hiding from your past never works. Take it from someone who knows firsthand—it will always come back to bite you. When I met Beth, I knew her family wouldn't accept a divorced man, so I didn't tell any of them until it was almost too late. I nearly lost the love of my life." Before Flynn could respond to the surprising admission, Ethan added, "Beth will be thrilled when she hears that the little girl she's fallen so in love with isn't going anywhere. So am I."

# CHAPTER TWENTY-THREE

Through sheer force of will, Cassie went back to work on building her candy Town Hall, even though she could barely concentrate when she had no idea how things were going between her father and Flynn.

Ethan Sullivan had always been protective of his daughters. And after Ashley got pregnant in high school, he'd taken it to new extremes.

Flynn was a million times stronger than the other guys she'd dated. But they'd only just agreed to give their relationship a chance...

At last, she heard the outside door open. She met Flynn halfway down the hall and was about to ask him how things had gone when his arms went around her and he was kissing her.

She could get used to this kind of greeting. Only, she still didn't know what his kiss meant. Was it good-bye? Or—

For several long moments, he kissed all thoughts out of her head, kissing her again and again and again.

Finally, he let her lips go for long enough that she

was able to ask, "What happened out there?"

"I told your dad everything. That my real name is Joe Miller. That I grew up in Centertown. That I left when I was seventeen and invented Flynn Stewart out of thin air."

"Oh my God, I can't believe you did that. You really *do* love me." She didn't realize what she'd said until it was too late. "I mean, I hoped that you did, but—"

"I love you, Cassie. So damned much." He kissed her again. "I should have said it to you before I told your dad."

Her head and heart were spinning faster and faster with every word from Flynn's beautiful mouth. *"You told my dad you love me?"*

"I might have taken a page out of your book and yelled it at him, actually."

Though Cassie had told him she loved him many times, it had never been to get him to say the words back. She simply needed him to know how she felt. But now that she knew he loved her too?

Cassie felt like she was standing beneath a beautiful rainbow while fireworks shot off and her favorite band played only for them.

Flynn stroked her cheek. "I also told your father that I'm not going to let him, or anyone else, get in the way of my loving you."

She didn't want to spoil the beautiful moment, but

she had to ask. "What about your past?"

He closed his eyes for a moment, clearly fighting the pull his past had over him. "I don't want to screw this up, Cassie. Not any of it. Not with you. Not with Ruby. Not with your family. But I won't lie to you either and say that I'm going to be able to change a lifetime of thinking, and behaviors, overnight."

"I'm not expecting you to do that, Flynn."

"You should. You shouldn't have to wait for me to catch up."

"Catch up?" She put her hand over his heart so that she could feel it beating strong and steady against her palm. "I'd say we're on pretty even ground right here, where it counts."

He went to kiss her again, but she beat him to it. It was tempting to get right to using the second little foil packet, but there was something she didn't want to forget to ask him first.

"I know you've been intent on keeping your anonymity here in Maine, but would you consider being my date for the awards ceremony in Portland tomorrow night?"

"I meant it when I told your father I'm not going to keep running. I don't know exactly how I'm going to come clean with everyone, or how many details I want to give about my past, but the one thing I do know is that I'd love to come to Portland to support you.

Although I'm guessing babies aren't on the guest list."

Emotion swamped her at the knowledge that Flynn was willing to risk dealing with the press—and their potentially intrusive questions about Ruby and her parentage—to support her. "I already asked Mom and my sisters if they could watch Ruby overnight. Just in case you were up for it." She squeezed his hand. "But I don't want you to come if you're not comfortable being away from Ruby for that long."

"If it were anyone but your mom and sisters, I wouldn't be. But Beth is already like the grandmother Ruby never had."

"Oh, she'll *love* hearing that."

"I still can't figure out what I've done to deserve you. Your family too."

"You don't have to do anything. Just be *you*."

"I'm trying to wrap my heart around the thought that life isn't one big bartering system. In Hollywood, that's how the game is played—you've got to give something to get something. And when I was a kid…" He shook his head. "It didn't matter what I tried to barter, nothing ever got any better. But when I'm with you—you're all my dreams, every fantasy I never thought could come true, all rolled into one."

Cupping her face in his hands, he gave her a kiss that was heartbreakingly gentle.

"Your love," he whispered, "is mine."

She smiled against his lips. "And your love is all mine."

* * *

Flynn knew Cassie had work to do, but that didn't make it any easier to force himself to leave. He was just walking out of her workshop when Beth texted to let him know Ruby had gone down for her nap a little early, if he wanted to take some extra time to work on his screenplay this morning.

Knowing it wasn't going to write itself, he headed back to the library for a second writing session. And as he opened his laptop, he could hardly believe it had been only a few hours ago that he had been sitting in this same chair.

It felt like his entire world had changed since then.

He loved Cassie.

And she loved him back.

Four weeks ago, he would have said that was impossible. He would have been certain that he could never trust anyone enough to let love either in or out. Even when Ruby had instantly vaulted over all his walls, he'd assumed it was because she was a defenseless baby. But then Cassie had followed her over, proving that love had found him not once, but twice.

Reading over the words he'd written that morning, he knew in his gut that he was finally on the right track. Ready to tell the truth not only to Ruby, and Cassie, and Ethan Sullivan, but to the whole world.

He put his fingers on the keyboard and let the words come.

*For Joe, walking into Cassie's house is like walking into a dream.*

*It's clean, for starters. It also smells so good, like all of Joe's favorite things to eat have just come out of the oven. Around the kitchen table, her brothers and sisters are playing and laughing. There is even a dog, a fluffy brown one who runs over and drops a ball at Joe's feet when they walk in.*

*"Everyone, this is Joe," Cassie calls out. She tells him her siblings' names, but he is so overwhelmed he knows he'll never remember them. "And this is my mom."*

*A light is shining behind Cassie's mom, so that when she smiles at him, she looks like an angel. "Hello, Joe. I'm so glad you could come home to play with Cassie today." She gestures to their sopping-wet clothes. "Looks like you two got caught in the rainstorm."*

*"It was fun!" Cassie laughs as she tells her mother, "We danced through the puddles all the way home."*

*He's never danced before, especially not in the rain, aiming for who could make the biggest splashes* in the puddles on the sidewalk.

"We'll show you our dance!" Cassie says.

Before Joe knows it, Cassie has grabbed his hands and is dancing with him in a circle, and he can't keep from laughing. She is so happy that she makes him feel happy too. Her mom claps her hands in time with their dance, even though they are making a mess on the floor.

"What talent you two have," she praises them when they finally tire out.

"I'm going to change into something dry," Cassie tells Joe. "Mom can find you something to wear, right, Mom?"

Cassie's mom nods. "Cassie's brothers have plenty of shirts and pants that should fit you, Joe. What do you say I get them for you while I dry your clothes?"

Joe is embarrassed by how dirty he is—not just his clothes, but his whole body. It's just that he doesn't have hot water where he lives, and it is so cold at night under just a dirty sheet that he doesn't want to get even colder by getting into an ice-cold bath.

As though she can read his mind, Cassie's mother says, "In fact, maybe it would be nice to warm up in the shower before changing?"

He nods, not sure he can trust his voice. But he wants to make sure she knows that he appreciates *how nice she is, so he says, "Thanks," even though it comes out kind of shaky.*

*"When you're both dry again," she adds, "I'll have snacks ready for you."*

*He feels his lip wobble then. No one has ever been this kind to him. Only today, with Cassie and her mom, has he ever felt like he mattered to anyone.*

*Fortunately, before Cassie's mom can see him cry, she leads the way toward the bathroom. He knows Cassie's siblings must be wondering what his deal is, but they don't stop what they're doing to stare. He'll have to face them and their questions soon, but Cassie will be with him by then.*

*Knowing she will make everything okay with her smiles, and her laughter, he finds himself wondering: If he spends enough time with her, can he learn how to be that happy too?*

★ ★ ★

That evening, after cooking dinner, giving Ruby a bath, reading her a book, then tucking her into her crib, Cassie and Flynn closed her bedroom door while she hummed softly to herself as she settled in for the night.

"Is there anything as good as cuddling with a warm, sleepy baby after she's had a bath?" Cassie asked.

Flynn drew her into his arms. "Only one thing I can

think of." He breathed in Cassie's sweet scent as he kissed her.

"Mmm, you're right," she agreed. "In fact, since we're talking about baths, what do you think about getting into one with me?"

Considering he'd had more than one fantasy about Cassie in the clawfoot bathtub, he was most definitely up for it. "What I think is that it's going to be one of the highlights of my life so far."

Taking his hand, she led him into the bathroom, pausing only to grab protection from her bedside table. She turned on the taps, and as the tub filled, he started to undress her. His hands weren't quite steady as he drew her shirt over her head and tossed it to the tiled floor, then unzipped her jeans and helped her step out of them. Her bra and panties came off next.

"*Gorgeous.*" He couldn't get his fill of looking at her. Nor could he be the slightest bit patient to have her as he lifted her into his arms with no warning, making her laugh as she wound her arms around his neck to hold on.

He lowered her into the tub, then ripped off his own clothes and was in the water with her sixty seconds later. Sitting against the far end of the tub, he floated her body over him so that she was straddling his hips.

"I know I'm supposed to be better with words than

this, but you really are *gorgeous*, Cassie."

"So are you." She traced one fingertip down the deep line between his abs. A teasing glint lit her eyes. "My Hollywood hunk." She could barely get the words out without giggling.

"Call me that again," he teased back, "and I won't be responsible for my actions."

Her eyes lit even further at his challenge. "My." She licked her lips. "Hollywood." She lowered her mouth to barely a breath from his. "Hunk."

He crushed her lips to his at the same time that he rocked his hips against hers, both of them gasping as her slick heat covered him. With his hands on her hips, he rotated her over him, water splashing around them as she drove him even crazier by rubbing her breasts over his chest.

The last thing he wanted was to pull away, but if he didn't put on protection in the next couple of seconds, Ruby might end up with a little brother or sister *really* soon. And though Flynn was surprised to realize that didn't sound at all bad, he would never make a huge life decision like that for Cassie without her consent.

After quickly putting on the condom, he threaded his hands into her hair, looked into her eyes, and said, "I love you." And then he showed her just how much he meant it with every stroke of his body inside of hers, with every caress of his hands over her slick skin, with every brush of his lips over hers.

As she arched back so that he could lave her breasts, he slid one of his hands between her thighs to intensify her pleasure. And as he watched her come apart, his name on her lips, he realized his dreams had all come true...and not a single one of those dreams had anything to do with the false pleasures of Hollywood or fame or the awards circuit.

Only the pure joy he felt in Cassie's arms.

★ ★ ★

Tucked up in bed together, Cassie had her head on Flynn's chest as he stroked the soft skin of her lower back.

"Thank you for the best day of my life," she murmured, her voice still pleasure-soaked and a little sleepy.

He pressed a kiss to the top of her head. "You took the words right out of my mouth."

Cassie had already given him more than he'd ever dreamed of. Her faith. Her laughter. Her love.

And yet...

He couldn't stop worrying that one wrong move on his part was all it would take to lose her.

She scooted up so that she could see his face in the moonlight. "I can read minds, you know." Though she spoke with a smile, he knew she was concerned. "Mostly because I'm pretty sure you're feeling the same way I am right now."

He wound a lock of her hair around his finger. He'd never done this—lain in bed talking, wanting to know all about the woman he was with. "What are you feeling?"

"So much love." She pressed a kiss to his lips. "But also a little fear. Not because I'm worried that you don't love me," she said before a bolt of panic could nail him in the center of his chest, "but because I've never cared this much about anything or anyone. If anything happened to you or Ruby..." The words choked up in her throat. "I never knew it could be the best day—and the scariest—simultaneously."

"How am I the one who makes my living with words, when you're the one who always says things best?" He drew her closer, her curves soft and perfect against his body as he finally admitted, "I'm terrified."

It helped to know he wasn't the only one who felt that way. That even someone as steady, as solid as Cassie could have a hard time finding her footing when the world shifted beneath her.

"Tonight when we were brushing our teeth," he continued, "I looked in the mirror and didn't recognize myself. I've never grinned like a fool while flossing. It's like you're rubbing off on me, in all the best ways. Not just in how happy you are, but how strong. Because only someone as strong as you can always find a reason to smile. To have the courage to put her heart on the line each and every day. To create so much beauty all around her."

"I'm learning from you too," she told him. "Learning how to fight for what I love. Learning how to keep moving forward even when it might seem easier to give up. Learning how to build a relationship that will last." She smiled before adding, "Not to mention learning how much fun it is to see you smile and hear you laugh—especially when we're making love."

"You're not the only one who loves that." In one quick move, she was on her back and he was levered over her.

She was already laughing by the time he nibbled the spot on her collarbone that he'd learned was ticklish. Soon, their laughter gave way to gasps and moans of pleasure as they surrendered to their desperate craving for each other, yet again. And when Cassie tumbled over the edge, Flynn went tumbling with her into sweet pleasure—and a startling sense of peace.

# CHAPTER TWENTY-FOUR

"You doing okay?" Cassie asked. "We can always go home if you're missing Ruby too much."

They'd been on the road for three hours, driving from Bar Harbor to Portland. Flynn had kept his phone on the dashboard in case Beth texted. The only messages that had come in, thankfully, were pictures of Ruby giggling with the dog and then playing drums with a spatula and a set of pots.

"I would never ask you to miss the awards ceremony," he replied as he pulled into valet parking in front of the hotel.

Cassie bit her lip. "What if *I'm* missing Ruby too much?"

He put the car in Park, then turned to put his hand on her cheek. "I love that you miss her as much as I do. But she's going to have the time of her life with your parents and siblings and Kevin while we're gone." He gave her a knowing smile as he added, "And you're not getting out of tonight that easily."

She sighed. "Have I mentioned how much I hate

standing up in front of a bunch of people?" Regardless of who won, at the end of the ceremony, all of the finalists would be called up to the stage in recognition of their achievements. She was already sweating just thinking about being in the spotlight.

"From your stories of the toasts and speeches you've given at Sullivan reunions and weddings and birthday parties and baby showers, it sounds like standing up in front of a bunch of people is exactly what you've been doing your whole life."

"It doesn't make me nervous if I'm related to them."

"In that case, instead of pretending they're all in their underwear while you're giving your acceptance speech, pretend they're long-lost Sullivans."

She laughed. "Honestly, there are so many of us all over the world that it isn't totally out of the realm of possibility."

The valet kept a discreet distance until Cassie opened her door. Jumping to service, he said, "Welcome to The Press Hotel. I will take care of your bags if you would like to go inside to check in."

Cassie had stayed at the boutique hotel once before, and she loved the rich history of the building in the Old Port district. "This building used to house the offices and printing plant of the *Portland Press Herald*," she told Flynn as they walked hand in hand through the elegant entry. "In fact, I read that one of the rooms has a fully restored 1925 Royal typewriter in it." If she hadn't become a candy confectioner, she very well might have been an antique specialist. Typewriters had always been a particular favorite.

"You don't see many buildings like this in California," he noted. "Everywhere I've been in Maine, there's such a sense of history."

She squeezed his hand, understanding everything he wasn't saying. Given that he'd left a small town for one of the biggest cities in the world, it meant so much to her that he had chosen to put down roots in another small town. Unlike in Los Angeles, he would never be able to disappear on a busy downtown street in Maine. Even Portland, while considerably bigger than Bar Harbor, was still tiny by Hollywood standards.

"Hello," she said to the woman behind the check-in desk. "I have a room reserved for one night under the name Cassie Sullivan."

"Welcome, Ms. Sullivan and—" The women did a double take when she looked at Flynn, not managing to cover her surprised reaction at coming face-to-face with a Hollywood celebrity.

But though Cassie could feel him stiffen, he didn't back away from the promise he'd made to stand by her side—and to face whatever fallout came from revealing that he had left Hollywood for Maine.

"Flynn Stewart."

Clearly flustered, the woman gave him a tremulous smile. "Mr. Stewart, sir, it's a pleasure to have you here. Both of you." The woman's fingers fumbled slightly on her keyboard as she pulled up their information on her screen. "I'm so pleased to see that the two of you have reserved the Penthouse Suite."

"I'm sorry," Cassie said with a shake of her head, "you must have my reservation mixed up with another visitor. I booked a standard room with a king bed."

"According to my records, you have been upgraded to our most exquisite suite of rooms. Your bags have already been sent up. I also see in the notes that you are a finalist for tonight's awards." She smiled as she handed Cassie the key to the Penthouse Suite. "Congratulations and best of luck. And please let us know if there is anything at all that we can do for you."

Cassie waited until they were alone in the elevator before asking Flynn, "Did you do that for us?"

He lifted her hand to his lips. "You deserve the best—and I intend to give it to you."

"You don't have to give me anything but yourself. But I'm not going to lie and say this isn't a *really* nice surprise."

She kissed him then and was still kissing him when the elevator opened on the seventh floor. A floor that had only one suite—theirs.

The surprises weren't over yet, because when she opened the door, she found champagne on ice and several gorgeous bouquets of her favorite flowers decorating the suite. "Oh Flynn...you are *such* a romantic."

She was about to kiss him again—and not stop this time—when she saw the antique typewriter she had mentioned to him only a few minutes ago. She read the note next to it out loud. *"We hope the panoramic views of Portland from the seventh floor or the journalism-rich history of the building inspire a letter, a poem, or short story during your time at The Press Hotel."* She grinned at Flynn. "Are you feeling inspired?"

"When I'm with you, *always*."

Though he hadn't told her anything about the new screenplay he was working on, she hoped it was true. Telling stories might have been a way to escape his past, but creativity was vital to Cassie's happiness in the present, and she knew the same went for Flynn.

Continuing their tour of the suite, they walked out on the rooftop patio, which had great views of the Old Port, the harbor, the surrounding islands, and the Atlantic Ocean.

"This is *beautiful*."

"Beyond beautiful," Flynn agreed.

When she realized he was looking at her rather than the view, she put her arms around him. "How about we go inside so that I can show you how much I appreciate all your thoughtful, romantic gestures? We should have just enough time before we need to get ready for the awards ceremony."

"Or we could save time by starting right here, right now." He lowered his mouth to the curve of her neck, nibbling on her sensitive skin.

"And risk indecent exposure?" She'd never contemplated doing something so risqué before.

"No one will see anything more than a couple kissing on a rooftop," he promised her. "Do you trust me, Cassie?"

She shivered, and not because it was cold. "Yes." She wrapped her arms tighter around him. "I trust you. With *everything*."

As though her response lit a fire inside of him, he crushed his mouth to hers, kissing her breathless. By the time he broke their kiss, he'd moved them to the outdoor couch.

Drawing her down to sit with him so that they were facing each other, he made sure his body blocked hers from any clear sight lines. If anyone looked out a window toward the rooftop terrace, they would see little more than Flynn's broad back.

"I'm glad you wore a dress today," he murmured as he slowly bunched the fabric in his hands.

The light stroke of his fingertips on her thighs as he

drew her dress higher made it impossible for her not to respond. She could only focus on the delicious sensation of his touch and the warmth of his breath on her skin as he pressed kisses from her earlobe to her collarbone.

"Your skin is so soft," he murmured between kisses. "You feel so good."

Her skirt was at her upper thigh when he finally slid his hand to the aroused flesh between her legs. Her breath was coming in gasps as one light touch, one perfect stroke of his fingers over silk, drove her straight to the edge. Again and again, he caressed her, and her eyes fell closed as she relished the sinfully sweet sensations.

"Look at me, Cassie." He momentarily stilled his hand. "I need to see you."

She opened her eyes to find his blazing with heat. And then—*oh God, it was so good*—he slid his hand over her bare skin, swallowing her cries of pleasure with his mouth as she climaxed.

Lifting her into his arms, he carried her inside the suite. In the bathroom, he turned on the shower, then stripped both of them out of their clothes. The glass-enclosed shower was all steamed up by the time they stepped inside, Flynn remembering to grab a condom at the last moment.

She ran her hands down his wet skin, the muscles

of his abdomen rippling beneath her touch. "I can't believe I get to live out my secret fantasies with you."

"Tell me one of your fantasies, Cassie, and we'll live it right now."

"We already are."

"You're one of the most creative people I've ever met." There was a sexy challenge in his eyes as he said, "You can do better than that."

She'd never felt more beautiful than she did with Flynn, but she'd never exactly been a sex goddess either. At least, not until he'd shown her that she had been one all along.

Slowly, she turned to face the tiled wall. Putting her hands flat on the cool tiles on either side of her head, she looked over her shoulder. "*This* is one of my fantasies."

She'd never seen his eyes so dark, or so hungry, as he drank her in. And then the hard, muscled length of his body was pressed along her backside, his hands and mouth seemingly everywhere at once. Cupping her breasts, caressing the curves of her hips, brushing against her lips—then starting at the top all over again, until she was writhing against him and begging him to take her.

At last, he sheathed himself, then gripped her hips in his big hands and drove into her in one powerful stroke. She cried out his name he took her to the peak of pleasure, then they catapulted into sheer bliss together.

Her legs were still trembling slightly as he gently washed her hair and body. It was the nicest thing in the world to be taken care of like this, by someone who clearly cherished her. By the time he turned off the water, then wrapped her in a plush towel, she felt more relaxed than she could remember.

"I'm not nervous about the awards ceremony anymore." She smiled as she added, "Mostly because I can't stop thinking about which fantasy I'm going to share with you once we come back to the room tonight."

★ ★ ★

Flynn needed a good ten minutes to get his body back under control after Cassie's comment about her *next* fantasy. When he finally won the battle with his arousal—as much as he could when, only a room away, Cassie was slipping into her dress and heels—he put on the black tuxedo he'd rented for the evening, then went out to the living room.

He was staring out over the moonlit Portland cityscape when he heard the click of heels on the hardwood floor. Turning to face Cassie, he had to put his hand on the glass to steady himself.

The sapphire-blue lace and silk slid over her curves

like a second skin. At once demure and breathtakingly sexy, it hinted at far more than it gave away. She had pulled her hair up into a loose bun and wore a pair of sparkling sapphire earrings that her mother had lent her for the evening. She also wore the four-leaf clover locket around her neck that her father had given her.

She looked like an angel.

His and Ruby's angel.

He took her hands in his. "You're the most beautiful woman I've ever seen."

Her smile was radiant. "And you're so handsome in your tux that I'm wondering if we can get away with being a little bit late to the ceremony."

"Don't worry," he promised, "I'll make waiting worth your while."

She licked her lips, looking sexier than ever as she asked, "How?"

He laughed, amazed by how natural it felt to laugh with Cassie, when it was something he'd rarely done before. "That's for me to know...and you to spend the next several hours anticipating." He was about to put his hand on the small of her back to guide her over to the door, when he could see that she obviously wasn't yet ready. "What is it, Cassie?"

"I know being my date tonight will probably open up a lot of questions about you and Ruby. Especially if any of the bigger media outlets cover the awards." She gripped his hands tightly. "But I'm going to make sure that no one ever hurts you or Ruby again. Not tonight. Not ever."

"I never knew someone could simultaneously be a fierce warrior *and* the sunniest person on the planet. Not until you." He kissed her gently. "And I'm not worried about anyone bothering me tonight. They're not going to be able to take their eyes off of *you*."

# CHAPTER TWENTY-FIVE

The hotel ballroom was a crush of people in glittering dresses and black tie. Flynn had been to many similar events in Hollywood, but this one felt completely different.

For starters, he wasn't here for his own gain. Tonight was all about Cassie. She'd shown him the work of her fellow finalists online, and while they were excellent confectioners, he remained confident that she would win. Every time one of her colleagues heaped her work with praise, he felt so damned proud and lucky to be standing beside her. What's more, while everyone in Hollywood competed with cutthroat intensity, these confectioners seemed very relaxed.

A half hour after their arrival, one of Cassie's friends pulled her away for a picture with several other finalists, leaving Flynn with the woman's husband. "You wouldn't happen to be Flynn Stewart, the screenwriter, would you?"

So far, no one had seemed to recognize him, and he'd been hoping he might make it through the whole night simply as Cassie's plus one. Flynn worked to keep his expression easy as he nodded. "I've written a few movies."

"I'm a *huge* fan." The guy looked like he couldn't believe his luck. "I know we're supposed to be keeping to small talk," he continued as Cassie and her friend returned, "but I've got to tell you how much of a difference your movies have made for me."

Before Flynn could say thank you, then change the subject, Cassie slipped her arm around his waist. "If you don't mind sharing," she said, "I'd love to know how Flynn's work has made a difference for you."

The other couple shared a look, their fingers threading together as the man said, "I had a terrible childhood, which I'm finally able to say out loud after years of therapy. But when I was still struggling, your movies were my go-to when I needed a boost. The way your heroes always manage to rise above their pasts, even when it seems impossible, made me feel I could do the same for myself."

Flynn was stunned. He hadn't realized he'd put so much of himself into his movies. Nor had he thought that his work would ever help anyone deal with something difficult in their past.

The master of ceremonies announced that it was time to take their seats for dinner, but before they did so, the other man shot him an apologetic look. "I didn't mean to put you on the spot. I just wanted to say thanks for doing such great work. I can't wait to see your next film."

"I knew it," Cassie said to Flynn once they were seated. "I knew anything you created would be beautiful. As beautiful as you are."

Before he could respond, the emcee greeted everyone. And as waiters circled the tables filling wine glasses and putting plates of food in front of them, Flynn deliberately pushed the man's comments into the back of his mind for the time being.

He'd never wanted anyone to win so badly. Cassie was so talented that her business would surely continue to grow by leaps and bounds without the award. Nonetheless, she deserved to know without so much as a flicker of doubt that she was the very best at what she did. Flynn, her siblings, her parents—they could tell her again and again that she was incredible, but it was still important for her to hear it from impartial judges.

Cassie wasn't the kind of woman who picked at her food, but she barely ate anything as the organizers gave a string of speeches, and then the cake and chocolate categories were awarded.

Finally, the candy category was up. Flynn clasped her hand tightly as the nominees were announced, their confections showcased on the large screen behind the podium. He would never have guessed so many innovative things could be done with candy—from lollipops that looked like little planets, to large blooms that looked exactly like flowers, to a three-foot-tall bear made entirely from sour straws.

"And the winner is…"

Though Cassie looked outwardly calm, she was nearly crushing Flynn's fingers while they waited. Out of the blue, Flynn was hit with a vision of the future where she gripped his hand as she gave birth to a little boy or girl.

Both the clarity of his vision—and his longing for it to come true—meant that he was nearly caught off guard when the presenter leaned into the microphone and said, "Cassie Sullivan!"

Cassie was clearly stunned as she remained in her seat, staring at the stage with wide eyes as the audience applauded her win.

Flynn put his hand gently on her cheek. "Congratulations, sweetheart."

His voice and touch snapped her out of her surprise. With her typical exuberance, she flung her arms around him. "I can't believe it."

"I can. You're amazing, Cassie. Never forget it."

She was positively glowing as she walked to the stage. Everyone she passed had a kind and congratulatory word for her. Flynn pulled out his phone to videotape her acceptance speech so that her family could see it all when they got back to Bar Harbor.

"Thank you." Holding the glass statue as tightly as she'd gripped his hand a moment before, she beamed at the audience. "I can't tell you how honored I am even to have been considered for this award. I admire each and every one of you so much, and I'm always hugely inspired by the work you do. Ever since I was a little girl, I've loved candy. Eating it, of course—" She grinned even wider as the room collectively laughed. "And making it in the kitchen with vats of sugar and food coloring and plenty of burning saucepans. Most parents would have worried about cavities and steered me in a more traditional direction. But my mother and father encouraged me to follow my dreams. This year, my siblings insisted I enter this competition. Love has always propelled me forward and given me a safe place to land." Cassie searched for Flynn in the audience. Her eyes were glittering with emotion as she said, "But never more than tonight, with the sweetest love of all."

In that moment, it was as though they were the only two people in the room. He mouthed, *I love you*, and Cassie gave him a radiant smile before turning her attention back to the room. "Thank you, again, for this honor."

All the nominees were brought up on stage as the emcee wrapped up the ceremony. The audience leaped to their feet as they applauded the talented group of confectioners.

When the house lights came up, Flynn went to find Cassie, who was being photographed with the other winners. While he didn't want to claim any part of her spotlight, he did want to make sure she knew he was there if she needed anything. As he watched her shine, not one of the models he'd dated over the years could compare. Cassie was the most stunning woman in the world, on every single level, inside and out.

And he was the luckiest guy in the world to get to be with her.

"Excuse me." A woman in a sharply tailored blue suit touched his shoulder. "Are you Flynn Stewart?"

He could spot an ambitious journalist from a mile away, one hungry enough for a scoop to turn any sound bite, no matter how small or irrelevant, to her advantage. His instinct was to shut the woman down and walk away. But he'd promised Cassie and her father—and himself—that he was done running.

"I am."

"You're here with Cassie Sullivan, is that correct?"

If she'd seen Cassie's acceptance speech, she knew damn well he was. "I am. Her work is extraordinary, isn't it?"

"Yes." The woman gave a cursory glance toward Cassie, who was standing beside her winning candy heart, surrounded by photographers. "I'm assuming her cousin Smith Sullivan is responsible for introducing you two?" Before he could reply, the woman looked around the room. "Is the baby here tonight?"

Flynn had never liked doing interviews. But that didn't mean he wasn't well aware of how the game was played. "Smith and Valentina are good friends," he said first, followed by a crystal clear, "My daughter is off-limits. Period."

"Of course," the journalist said, slightly chastened.

He knew it wouldn't last, though. Not when there was a major scoop to be had. Just as he was about to shift the conversation to Cassie's brilliant work, she broke away from her photo call and slipped her hand into his.

"Hello, I'm Cassie." She extended her other hand to the journalist.

"Jasmine Gordon from the *Portland Press Herald*. Congratulations on your win."

"Thank you." Cassie's smile was sweet as could be as she said, "If you don't mind my stealing Flynn away, I need his assistance backstage."

The journalist hesitated before nodding—and pressing a card into Flynn's hand. "If there's anything you'd like to share with your fans, I'm available to talk whenever it works for you."

Cassie waited to speak again until she had pulled him into the deserted backstage area. She looked fiercely protective as she asked, "What did she say to you?"

Flynn responded with a kiss. He'd told Cassie she didn't have to fight his battles for him, but she'd been adamant that he shouldn't have to fight them alone. Fighting them together was a new concept for him, but one he found he really liked.

"I love you, Cassie."

"I love you too." She wrapped her arms around him. But then she scowled. "I'm serious—do I need to give that woman a piece of my mind?"

"No." He kissed the scowl from her lips. "She's just doing her job."

"I know you want tonight to be all about me," Cassie said softly. "And I love you even more for that. But I meant it when I told you I won't let anyone hurt you or Ruby."

"They won't," he promised her. "Talking with the journalist made me realize, yet again, how imperative it is to finally come clean. The longer I hide the truth about Ruby—and myself—the more the press will probe. I've spent the past twenty years feeling hunted. I refuse to have either you or Ruby feel that way. Just as I refuse to let my past get in the way of your win tonight. The world is yours, Cassie. And nothing would make me happier than seeing you grab it with both hands."

"Well, if it will make you happy..." At last, her lips turned up at the corners in that beautiful smile he so loved to see. "Let's go grab the world." She lifted his hands to her lips. "Together."

\* \* \*

Cassie sparkled all night long. Even when she'd been ready to duke it out with the journalist, she hadn't lost her glow. Hours later, when they were back in their suite, Flynn could see how tired she was.

He led her over to the couch in the living room. "Time for you to relax." Once she was seated, he slipped off her shoes, then rubbed the soles of her feet.

A blissful smile on her face, she closed her eyes and leaned her head against the plush cushions. "I may never let you stop doing that."

"Anything you want, consider it yours."

She opened one eye to look at him. "Do you really mean that?"

"Of course I do."

"Well, that's good, because..." She bit her lip. "I want to watch one of your movies tonight."

He nearly dropped her foot, he was so surprised. "Why would you want to do that?"

"Why *wouldn't* I, when everyone who has seen them has raved about how great they are?" Before he could protest, she added, "I know you said you never wanted me to see one, but I was hoping you might be persuaded to change your mind about that. Plus, the TV in here is so huge it will be almost like watching it in the theater—and they've even left us microwave popcorn and Milk Duds."

Flynn hadn't yet unpacked the man's comments from earlier about how his thrillers had helped him deal with a bad childhood. Could that be right? Could Flynn have been wrong about the worth of his own work?

"Okay."

She threw her arms around him. "Thank you." Too soon, however, she was moving away. "I love Lola's dress, but I'm dying to put on leggings and a T-shirt. Be right back."

Flynn worked to squash his apprehension over what they were about to do as he put the popcorn in the microwave. Millions of people had seen his movies, but no one's opinion had ever mattered so much before. If Cassie didn't like what she saw—

He was so lost in his head that the microwave had beeped a good half-dozen times by the time Cassie reappeared beside him and pulled out the steaming bag.

"You don't have to worry," she said, reading his mind. "I'm going to love it." She tugged him back to the couch, turned on the TV, then typed his name into the search box for the streaming service. "Do you want to choose, or should I just pick one at random?"

Flynn's nerves were choking him so tightly that he could barely get out the words, *"The Dark Drive."*

From the first note of the soundtrack, Cassie was clinging to Flynn. By the time the seventeen-year-old protagonist walked on-screen, she was watching the movie through the fingers of the hand she'd put over her eyes. If they had been watching someone else's movie, the little yelps she gave every few minutes might have made him laugh. Tonight, he was too busy praying she wouldn't hate his work to find anything the least bit funny.

Surprisingly, he soon found himself caught up in the movie. Though he'd written the twists and turns, the director and actors were so good at their craft that Flynn was almost surprised by the plot a couple of times.

But what surprised him far more than the tense, dramatic beats of the movie was the fact that the hero of the film really *was* a hero. Beaten and bruised, he still managed to rise up from defeat and beat back the villain *and* his own fears and insecurities.

There were tears in Cassie's eyes when the credits rolled. "I loved it." She wiped the wetness from her cheeks as she said, "I mean, it was *terrifying*. But so empowering. I swear, I feel like I could vanquish all the bad guys now."

He drew her onto his lap. "Don't you know? You already have."

Their lips met in a kiss that was so much more than attraction, that went so much deeper than desire. And as they tumbled together into ecstasy, it was love—and the sweetest possible joy—at the heart of every caress and every sigh of pleasure.

# CHAPTER TWENTY-SIX

Cassie was sleeping soundly when Flynn slipped out of bed several hours later. Moonlight streamed through the window, illuminating her face. Even in sleep, her lips curved up at the corners. Whether because of their lovemaking—or because of her big win—he didn't know. All that mattered was that she was happy. He vowed to spend the rest of his life making sure of it.

After her win tonight, he had no doubt that her career was going to grow like crazy. He planned to stand beside her and help out in whatever way he could during the climb.

Flynn had lived through his own dizzying career climb, only to find himself facing the unknown, a future he could no longer clearly define. He'd been so certain his thrillers weren't worth watching, only to belatedly realize he'd imbued them with more meaning than he'd been willing to face all these years. Maybe, just maybe, it wasn't impossible to think of writing another.

But for now, there was a project he wanted to pour

his heart and soul into.

Carrying the antique typewriter over to the dining table where he could still see Cassie sleeping soundly, but where he wouldn't wake her with the pounding of the keys, he slid in a fresh piece of paper and let the words spill from his heart onto the page.

*After dinner at Cassie's house, Joe's belly isn't the only thing that's full. He's never been around a dinner table where everyone is talking at once, where the dad isn't drunk or high, where the mom laughs just as much as the kids. It's been the greatest night of his life—the greatest day, full stop—but somehow that only makes knowing he has to go home worse.*

*"Are you ready to meet Ellie the elephant?" Cassie is bouncing up and down on her toes, she's so excited.*

*He already looked in the backyard and didn't see any elephants, especially ones with polka dots. But even if Cassie really does have an elephant hiding somewhere, it's too late for Joe to see it now.*

*"It's almost dark. I've got to get home." His sister will be hungry. And probably scared too, wondering where he is.*

*His stomach hurts. He should never have been so selfish as to come to Cassie's house. What if something happened to his sister while he wasn't there to protect her?*

*"You could sleep over," Cassie offered. "I already asked, and Mom and Dad said that would be awesome."*

*"I can't." They're the hardest words he's ever spoken, when spending the night in this happy home is literally his biggest dream. He's heading for the front door, planning to sprint all the way home, when Cassie's mom stops him.*

*"Is everything okay? Do you want to spend the night here with us?"*

*"You've been so nice." His lips wobble again. "I wish I could stay," he admits to Cassie's mom. He feels he can tell her anything and she won't yell at him. "But I can't."*

*"Joe." She puts her hand on his shoulder, the most tender touch he's ever felt from a grown-up's hand. "If there's anything you need help with, anything you need to talk about, I'm here and happy to help. So is Cassie's dad."*

*He wants so badly to tell her everything, about being hungry and dirty and cold and worried all the time. But all that comes out is, "My little sister gets scared without me."*

*"How lovely that you have a sister. What's her name?"*

*"Sarah."*

*"What a pretty name. I'd love to meet her." Her eyes widen as though an idea has just come to her.*

*"Why don't I drive you home?"*

*"No." He spits out the word. He can't stand the thought of Cassie's mom seeing where he lives. "I can walk."*

*But for all her smiles and laughter and delicious cooking, Cassie's mom is no pushover. "I insist. Honey?" She calls over to her husband, who is standing in the kitchen doorway watching their conversation. "Why don't we take Joe home?"*

*"I want to come too," Cassie says.*

*Cassie's mother and father share a look. "Perfect," her mom says a beat later, "we'll need your voice for harmony in the car."*

*"Why is there harmony in your car?" Joe asks.*

*Cassie's mom winks at him. "You'll see."*

*Joe slides into the backseat of the nicest-smelling, cleanest car he's ever been in. There's a doll, a baseball, and some socks on the floor, but there are no smears of dirt, no packages of half-eaten fast food that have been rotting for weeks, no cigarette butts.*

*Cassie's dad starts the engine, and a song starts playing. One that everyone knows well enough that they all sing along, something about having twenty thingamabobs.*

*"Do you know this song?" Cassie asks. "It's from* The Little Mermaid.*"*

*Joe shakes his head.*

*"Oh, I can't wait to show you! You're going to love it! It's about this mermaid who wants to see what it's like to live on land, and all these amazingly cool things happen to her. It's Ellie's favorite movie."*

*"Your elephant?"*

*Cassie nods like it's the most normal thing in the world for an elephant to have a favorite movie, not to mention being covered in polka dots and living somewhere in her house.*

*Before he can express his doubt, they're heading into the woods.*

*"I've never been here before," Cassie says.*

*Her mother smiles at them over her shoulder, but Joe is so attuned to adult moods that he can see the concern behind her upturned lips. His stomach clenches tighter and tighter the closer they get to his house.*

*Too soon, they're parked outside the ramshackle building. Half the roof is covered with a tarp, while the shingles on the other half are rotting.*

*He's horribly embarrassed. And also afraid of what's going to happen next.*

*His father stumbles out on the porch and bellows, "Who the hell is trespassing on my property?" His beer belly hangs over the waistband of his dirty jeans, and his shirt doesn't cover all of it.*

*"Stay in the car for now, kids," Cassie's dad*

*says, then he and Cassie's mom get out.*

But Joe can't stand the thought of his dad hurting them. No one has ever been so nice to him. They don't deserve to suffer at his father's hands.

Joe throws himself out of the car. "It's my fault," he calls out to his father. "I got lost on the way home from school, and they offered to drive me home." He hates lying in front of Cassie and her parents, but telling this lie is the only way he knows to keep them safe.

"Lost?" His father sneers at him, but when he starts forward, he stumbles and has to reach out a hand to steady himself on the side of the house. "You really are dumb as a rock if you're getting lost coming to your own house."

"He's not dumb!" Cassie calls out. "Joe is smart and fun, and I like him."

Joe's father tries to focus on Cassie. "Who the hell are you?" His words are getting more slurred by the second.

Cassie's mom is standing between Cassie and Joe now, putting one arm around each of them. It's the first time Joe has ever felt even the slightest bit safe around his father.

"Joe is going to be spending the night at our house," she informs his father. "We're here to pick up Sarah too."

Joe's mother stumbles out then, half dressed,

*with mottled bruises in different stages up and down her legs and arms. There's one on her neck too, and seeing it makes Joe shudder. "Who are they?"*

*"Doesn't matter." Joe's father gestures to him. "Get the hell in here, boy. We're hungry, and you need to get cooking."*

*But Cassie's dad is already pushing past Joe's parents to get into the house and get Joe's sister out. When Joe's dad tries to stop him, Joe races past.*

*"Sarah, where are you?" he calls. She'll tell him once she hears his voice. Joe finds her hiding in the closet, their usual hiding place when their parents are drunk and on a rampage. "It's okay, we don't have to stay here tonight. Cassie's parents asked us to sleep over at their house."*

*"Who's Cassie?"*

*Sarah is little for her age, looking closer to five than eight. But she trusts Joe. She still believes that he has the power to make everything better. He never wants to let her down.*

*His heart is pounding like crazy as he tells her, "Cassie is my friend."*

*It's the bravest thing he's ever done, daring to claim someone as wonderful as Cassie as a friend. But he knows it's true. Knows that even though they've only just met, she'll always be there for him. Knows that even on the rainiest day, her smile will be brighter than the sun.*

"Can I bring my puppy?" Sarah whispers.

When Joe nods, she gets the stuffed dog out of its hiding place beneath one of the floorboards in the closet. It's the only toy their parents haven't completely destroyed or gotten rid of in a rage.

"Let's go." He holds out his hand, and when his sister takes it, he can't stop himself from hugging her. He would never want to leave without her, can't imagine how horrible it would be to leave her behind.

"What's Cassie's house like?" she asks.

"It's the best place in the whole world," he tells her.

When they get out to the porch, they find Cassie's father holding theirs against the wall, one hand on his chest, the other trapping his hands behind his back. Though Joe's dad is trying to fight him off, Cassie's dad is barely breaking a sweat keeping him in place.

"You leave, boy, and you ain't ever coming back!" Joe's father is furious. "Same goes for you, girl. We ain't ever spending another penny on you."

Joe swallows hard. This place, this life, is all he's ever known. He wants to leave, but still, it's hard. Hard to step into the unknown. Hard to go someplace new, where he's worried he'll disappoint everyone the same way his parents say he disappoints them.

*That's when Cassie comes to take his hand. "You're so brave, Joe. You can do anything you want to do." She smiles at Sarah. "So are you. I'm Cassie."*

*His sister gives Cassie a shy smile. "I'm Sarah." And then, "Do you really think I'm brave?"*

*"So brave!" She takes Sarah's hand and tugs them both toward the car. "Let's go so that I can introduce you to Ellie before lights-out."*

*"Who's Ellie?" Sarah is remarkably resilient, cowering in the closet one moment and chatting with Cassie the next.*

*"My elephant."*

*Sarah's eyes are huge. "You have an elephant?"*

*"I do," Cassie says with a smile. "And she can't wait to meet you both."*

*Joe is still reeling from the confrontation with his father. But focusing on Cassie's smile, and the warmth of her hand in his, makes him feel a million times better.*

*When they get back to Cassie's house, Sarah wolfs down some leftovers from dinner, takes a bath, dresses in a pair of jammies that belong to Cassie's younger sister, then joins Cassie and Joe in a fort they've made out of couch pillows and bed sheets in the living room.*

*Sarah's eyes are big as she takes it in. "This really is the best place in the whole world."*

"It gets even better!" Cassie promises. She gives them each a flashlight and tells them to turn it on before crawling out of the fort on her hands and knees. A few seconds later, the lights go out. They hear her giggling as she comes back across the room. "Mom made cookies!" she announces, and Sarah doesn't hesitate to dive on the plate full of chocolate chip cookies.

But Joe's stomach is too full of butterflies to eat right now. Being with Cassie is like every dream he never thought would come true. She's funny and pretty, and she isn't scared of anything. Not even his dad. He's never going to forget the way she defended him and said he was smart.

"Are you ready to meet Ellie the elephant?" Cassie's eyes are bright, and she looks so excited.

Sarah nods, looking so full of joyful anticipation that Joe's chest feels tight inside. "I am!"

With great flair, Cassie reaches under one wall of their fort and slides a cardboard box inside. Looking into the open top, Joe can see that it's decorated with the wild grasses of Africa. That is, if the grasses were every color of the rainbow.

Standing in the middle of the box is a stuffed elephant. It has pink and purple polka dots all over it—and Joe can't help but grin as he looks at it.

"Hello, I'm Ellie." Cassie has changed her voice so that it sounds like an animated character instead *of her, making Sarah laugh. She's also lifted up the elephant so that it looks like it's walking on air. "I've been waiting to meet you guys. Want to go on an adventure with me and my friend Cassie?"*

*"Yes!" Sarah claps her hands. "Me and Joe love adventures."*

*Joe and Sarah have always made up stories to-gether. Disappearing into a pretend world, hiding out in the woods, pretending they are knights and princesses and pirates are their favorite things to do together.*

*Now that Cassie and her stuffed elephant are in the mix, it doesn't feel like pretend anymore. And when the three of them make up a story about two girls named Sarah and Cassie and a boy named Joe, he can see the scenes in his head so clearly. He keeps his eyes closed as they each take turns making up parts of the adventure. It's like watching a movie. At one point when Joe hears laughter, he's surprised to realize it's coming from him.*

*When the story comes to a conclusion that has all of them laughing so hard they're rolling around holding their bellies, Joe knows that for the rest of his life, he'll never forget this night. Because it has been the best one ever.*

*Though he doesn't want to miss out on any new adventures, he has to go to the bathroom. He scoots out of the fort and is halfway across the living room* when he hears Cassie's parents talking in the kitchen.

"It was even worse than I thought." From where he's standing, he can see how sad her mother looks. "We can't let them go back there."

Her father looks sad too, but determined. "We won't."

Joe can hardly believe what he's hearing. All day long, he's been trying to soak up every great moment, because he knows nothing this good can possibly last.

Is it possible that Cassie's parents might really want to keep them?

"No matter how hard we have to fight for Joe and Sarah," her father says as if in answer to Joe's silent question, "we're not going to let them down."

That's when they see him eavesdropping. "I'm sorry," he blurts, "I didn't mean to be a snoop."

"You weren't snooping," Cassie's dad reassures him. They both get up and walk over to him. "We were just talking about how we want you and Sarah to come live with us permanently. Would you like to be a part of our family?"

Again, he's afraid to admit how badly he wants that. If he gets his hopes up and then it doesn't happen, of all the bad things he's already lived through, it would be the worst.

He's lied so many times to protect himself and

*his sister, that he's about to lie again by telling them he doesn't care.*

*But then he hears Sarah laughing in the fort with Cassie...and remembers Cassie saying how brave he is.*

*Can it be true? All these years, has he actually been brave?*

*Brave enough to shield his sister from the worst of it.*

*Brave enough to keep going when anyone else would have given up.*

*Brave enough to accept an invitation from Cassie to meet an elephant...and enter a world beyond his wildest imaginings.*

*And if all those things are true, then can it also be true that he doesn't have to be brave all by himself anymore? That he can be a part of a real family and say how he really feels without being scared?*

*Joe takes a deep breath before looking up at Cassie's mom and dad and taking the biggest risk of his life. "Yes, I want us to be part of your family."*

*"I'm so happy," Cassie's mom says, and he can see the joy plainly written on her face. "Can I hug you?"*

*When he nods, she wraps her arms around him. It's so nice. As nice as when Cassie was pushing him on the swing and he felt like he was flying. As nice as splashing in puddles beside his new friend. As* nice as making up stories with Sarah and Cassie about Ellie the elephant.

But though Cassie's mom says she's happy, she's also crying. He can tell by the way her shoulders are shaking.

"Don't worry, honey," she says before he can worry that he's done something wrong. "These are happy tears."

Happy tears seem as impossible as an elephant taking three kids on a great adventure in the living room. And yet, Joe was there, wasn't he? On a breathless and exciting journey with Sarah and Cassie—and Ellie the elephant.

The adventure is still fresh in his mind's eye when Joe finally understands what Cassie has known all along: Anything really is possible.

# CHAPTER TWENTY-SEVEN

Neither Cassie nor Flynn could wait to get home to Ruby. So instead of lingering over breakfast in their suite the next day, they hit the road bright and early. The Sunday morning traffic was sparse enough for them to make it back to Bar Harbor in record time. As soon as Flynn parked the car in front of her parents' house, they practically sprinted up the walkway.

Cassie's dad met them at the door, holding Ruby in his arms. The baby gave a happy cheer as she reached out her arms to Flynn and Cassie. They reached out to take her from Ethan. Together, the three of them did a sweet group hug.

As soon as he could, Cassie's father pulled her into a hug of their own. "Congratulations, honey. Your mother and I are both so proud of you."

"Thanks, Dad." She gave him an extra big squeeze, loving him even more for the way he'd welcomed Ruby and Flynn into his life. "Winning was such a surprise."

"Only to you," Flynn said as he settled Ruby on his

hip. When the baby lifted Ellie the elephant to his lips, he gave her stuffed toy a kiss. "We all knew you were going to win."

Cassie had repeatedly asked Flynn to recognize how special his work was. Now she found herself wondering whether it was time for her to take a closer look at her own.

"Come on in," Ethan said. "We were just about to sit down to lunch. Your mom thought you might be back early, so she made enough for all of us." He ran an affectionate hand over Ruby's hair. "This little treasure is hard to leave for too long, isn't she?"

"We nearly turned back yesterday," Cassie admitted as they headed into the kitchen.

"Welcome back!" Beth was serving up a mouthwatering Guinness beef and onion potpie for the four of them, along with sweet potato puree for Ruby. "I hope you're hungry."

"Starved," Cassie said as she carried the plates over to the table. Between being too nervous to eat last night and making love repeatedly with Flynn, she felt as though she could eat *all* the potpie by herself.

"Thank you for watching Ruby." Flynn smiled at her parents. "And thanks for texting over so many pictures while we were gone. She obviously had the time of her life here."

"All of us did," Beth said as they sat down to eat.

"Now, tell us about last night. Was it absolutely wonderful?"

Cassie could feel her cheeks grow pink as she flashed back to all the wonderfully sexy parts of her night with Flynn. Fortunately, he stepped in with a response before her parents could notice.

"Cassie was the star of the evening." Flynn pulled out his phone and showed them the video. "As soon as we walked in, everyone wanted to talk with her. And you've never heard such loud cheering as when she won. Your daughter is magnificent."

Though Flynn was answering her mother's question, he was looking at Cassie as he spoke. She couldn't look away from him either. Just as she couldn't stop hoping that one day he'd realize how magnificent *he* was.

For the rest of their meal, Cassie and Flynn answered questions about the awards ceremony. It wasn't until their plates were empty that her father cleared his throat.

"Have you seen the Sunday paper yet?" He brought it over to the table. "They covered the awards on the front page."

"Lola is going to be very pleased," Beth said as she pointed to the large picture of Cassie wearing the dress her sister designed.

But Cassie was far more concerned about Flynn's

reaction to the article, which mentioned him—along with the mystery surrounding his adoption of Ruby and his subsequent disappearance from Hollywood—several times. It also speculated on his relationship with Cassie and the Sullivan family as a whole.

"Beth, Ethan, I'm sorry for bringing your family into my mess."

Beth put her hand on Flynn's arm. "Families can be messy. We Sullivans know that better than anyone. You have nothing to apologize for. Not now or in the future."

"Unless you do anything to hurt Cassie," Ethan put in.

*"Dad!"* Cassie exclaimed at the same time Beth said, *"Ethan!"*

But Flynn didn't look at all put out by her father's ongoing protectiveness. "You have my word that I never will, sir."

And when her father smiled, Cassie could see that Ethan Sullivan's approval meant the world to Flynn.

★ ★ ★

They took Ruby to the park before heading home. Flynn put her in the baby swing, and as he gave her a push, she laughed and happily kicked her feet in the air. Cassie pretended to tickle her feet every time she came close, making Ruby giggle even harder.

Cassie grinned at Flynn. "What a happy little girl you have."

"She really is, isn't she?"

Cassie knew Flynn would never take happiness for granted. Every moment of joy for Ruby, and for himself, would always be incredibly precious.

Just then, a young mother came to the park with twins, a boy and girl who looked to be close to Ruby's age. She settled them in the sandbox with bright plastic shovels and buckets to play with.

When Ruby kept staring at them, Cassie said, "Looks like she wants to make new friends."

Flynn seemed momentarily uncertain, which Cassie guessed had to do with the perils of his own childhood. Yet again, she hoped that one day soon, when he felt ready, he'd share more of his past with her.

When it was clear just how much Ruby wanted to play, he moved to unstrap her. Together, they took Ruby over to the sandbox.

"This is Ruby," he said to the twins' mom. "Could she play in the sandbox with your children?"

"Sure." The woman smiled. "The more the merrier. Iris and Rob love other kids."

Cassie could see that Flynn was still a little nervous about how Ruby was going to do with the other babies. Fortunately, after a few seconds of eyeballing each other, the little boy handed Ruby his blue shovel and was already obviously half in love with her as the three kids made a joyful mess of themselves in the sand.

Cassie loved seeing not only how happy Ruby looked, but also the joy on Flynn's face as he finally relaxed into the knowledge that, despite his and his sister's harrowing childhood, Ruby was going to be just fine.

* * *

In the cabin an hour and a half later, they had just put Ruby down for a nap when Flynn said, "I'd like you to read what I've been working on."

Cassie's heart had never felt fuller than it did when she took the folder from him. "I'd love to." But before she began, she needed to be certain about something. "Are you sure you're ready to share this with me? I don't want to get in the way of your creative process."

She'd never seen him look so serious, so intense, as he did when he told her, "You're the reason I was able to write it. So yes, I'm sure."

On the couch, she began to read.

*Ellie the elephant is born in a factory in upstate New York…*

By the fifth sentence, she was holding her breath.

By the tenth, her eyes were welling up. By the time she read the final words—*Anything really is possible*—tears were running down her cheeks.

Slowly, Cassie put the pages back inside the folder. While she'd been reading, Flynn had stood perfectly still by the window, staring out at the metal heart on the tree trunk.

She walked across the room and put her arms around him, resting her cheek on his back. "It's beautiful, Flynn. Every single word. Thank you for sharing your story with me."

He turned, sliding one hand around her waist, wiping away her tears with the other.

She wouldn't lie and tell him they were all happy tears. How could they be, when he'd given her a clear window into his horrible childhood? But that wasn't all he'd done with the story.

He'd not only shown her his past, he'd also written the beautiful beginnings of their love story. One in which he finally learned how to laugh again.

"It's all true, isn't it?" Cassie asked.

Of course she understood where fact and fiction diverged: It was the underlying emotion in his story that she was referring to. Joe's fear of his parents, his alienation from his peers, the warm welcome and support from Cassie's family, and most of all his boundless love for his sister.

And for her.

"It is. All my adult life, I've deliberately looked at everything through my writing lens so I could stay at a distance, without having to acknowledge how I personally felt. But with you, though I said at first I wanted to learn about you for a character sketch, it was just another lie. I wanted to know everything I could about you because you captured my heart. Something I never thought would happen..." He stroked her cheek. "Even as I was writing this, I asked myself what the hell I knew about creating a love story. But then I realized that you taught me everything I needed to know about love simply by the way you immediately loved Ruby without reservation, without hesitation, without boundaries."

"That's exactly how you loved Sarah. The way you'll always love her."

Flynn tightened his hold around Cassie as he nodded. "Sarah and I were so close when we were kids. We looked out for each other. We took care of each other. And we made up stories together. Writing about her..." He swallowed hard. "It was like having her back for a little while. Before everything got so totally screwed up. Before I lost her completely."

"Sarah will never be gone completely. She'll always live on in Ruby."

"Sometimes," he said in a low voice, "when I look

at Ruby, it feels like I'm looking at Sarah. It hurts…but it's also good to know that she'll never truly be gone. And when Ruby was playing so happily with the other kids in the park today, it finally hit me that the cycle of pain and sorrow and shame is broken. It's what Sarah would have wanted for her daughter, I'm sure of it."

"I'm sure of it too," Cassie said. "Just as I'm sure that if I had known your sister as a child, I would have liked her. A lot."

"She would have liked you too. How could she not, when even a grumpy Hollywood cynic fell for you the moment you gave him a big smile and said hello?"

"You weren't the only one who fell in love at first sight." Cassie needed him to know this. "I tried to tell myself it was only Ruby who captured my heart that quickly, but the first time I heard you say *I love you* to Ruby, I had to admit how deep my feelings ran for you too. And loving you has also helped me accept the truth about what I do. That I'm not just playing around with candy, but that there is so much heart and soul— and worth—in my work."

"You spread joy in everything you do, Cassie. That's worth *everything*."

Their lips met in a kiss that echoed their words of love.

"I wish I could tell you it's going to be smooth sailing from here," Flynn said. "But I can't predict how people will react when I tell my story—the real one, this time." He cupped her face in his hands. "Maybe a better man wouldn't ask you to take on everything that comes with me and my past *and* raising a precocious six-month-old."

"Ask me, Flynn." It was what he'd said to her the night he'd finally told her the truth—and declared his love.

"Will you take us on?" Deep emotion reverberated through his words. "Will you love us and let us love you back with everything we are?"

*"Yes! Yes! Yes!* I'm yours, Flynn. Body, heart, and soul." Cassie's love for Flynn and Ruby ran so deep that she was confident they could withstand whatever the world—and the press—tried to throw at them. "And it doesn't matter how people react to the truth of your past. All that matters is that you feel good about whatever you choose, or choose not to, share."

"That's something I've been thinking about a lot. Not only how to come clean *and* show Ruby how special her mother was, but also how to help kids who are having a rough time. I know that guy we met at the awards ceremony said my thrillers helped him deal with his rotten childhood, but I keep thinking that a story about three kids who create fantastic adventures for themselves could reach children while they're still young. Before they forget how to hope and dream and laugh. Because if they see a character that's like them on the screen, maybe they'll realize they aren't alone." She could see the determination—and the excitement—in his eyes. "I'd like to bring Sarah and Joe to life on-screen. And little Cassie too, if it's okay with you."

"It's more than okay. It will be *amazing* to see your stories about these kids on the screen. I love it." She kissed him. "I love you." She kissed him again. "And I can't wait to be beside you every step of the way."

"Someone very wise once told me all I needed to do was take one small step forward at a time, until I was where I wanted to be." He moved closer to her at the exact moment that she did the same. "And now here I am, with you."

# EPILOGUE

*Six months later...*

Most woodworkers avoided hand-sanding whenever possible. For Rory Sullivan, however, sanding his furniture by hand was mandatory. He might never achieve perfection, but that didn't stop him from trying.

It was one of the main things Rory's mother and father had taught him and his six siblings—to always give their all. Whether they won or lost, the most important thing was that they'd done their very best.

Rory was glad to see Cassie's hard work paying off. In the wake of her award, she'd been commissioned to create a large art piece for a museum exhibition in Japan, along with several lucrative private commissions. Rory couldn't be happier for his sister. She deserved all the good fortune coming her way—as did her boyfriend, Flynn.

Though Rory hadn't been sure about the guy at first, by the time Cassie moved into her cabin to live with Flynn and Ruby, her new boyfriend had proved himself in spades. Not only by treating Cassie extremely well, but also by having the guts to tell his story to the world.

During the past six months, Flynn had worked with Smith and Valentina at Sullivan Studios to put together a part live-action, part animated short film inspired by Flynn's rough childhood and the people who helped him transcend it. The film was already shortlisted for several awards, but what impressed Rory most was how Flynn had bravely uncovered his secrets, both with the film and then with the interviews he'd done to support it. Cassie and Ruby had been by his side throughout, of course. Rory could hardly remember a time when the three of them weren't a tight unit.

Whistling sounded from outside the open barn doors to his woodshop, pulling Rory from his thoughts and making him grind his teeth. Whistling had never irritated him before.

Not until Zara.

She always looked at him the same way, like she knew all of *his* secrets. And though that was impossible, he couldn't shake the feeling that one day, if he wasn't fully on guard around her, she just might find a way to break through his barriers and see what he was hiding...

## ABOUT THE AUTHOR

Having sold more than 8 million books, Bella Andre's novels have been #1 bestsellers around the world and have appeared on the *New York Times* and *USA Today* bestseller lists 86 times. She has been the #1 Ranked Author on a top 10 list that included Nora Roberts, JK Rowling, James Patterson and Steven King, and Publishers Weekly named Oak Press (the publishing company she created to publish her own books) the Fastest-Growing Independent Publisher in the US. After signing a groundbreaking 7-figure print-only deal with Harlequin MIRA, Bella's "The Sullivans" series has been released in paperback in the US, Canada, and Australia.

Known for "sensual, empowered stories enveloped in heady romance" (Publishers Weekly), her books have been Cosmopolitan Magazine "Red Hot Reads" twice and have been translated into ten languages. Winner of the Award of Excellence, The Washington Post called her "One of the top writers in America" and she has been featured by Entertainment Weekly, NPR, USA Today, Forbes, The Wall Street Journal, and TIME Magazine. A graduate of Stanford University, she has given keynote speeches at publishing conferences from Copenhagen to Berlin to San Francisco, including a standing-room-only keynote at Book Expo America in New York City.

Bella also writes the *New York Times* bestselling "Four Weddings and a Fiasco" series as Lucy Kevin. Her sweet contemporary romances also include the USA Today bestselling Walker Island and Married in Malibu series written as Lucy Kevin.

If not behind her computer, you can find her reading her favorite authors, hiking, swimming or laughing. Married with two children, Bella splits her time between the Northern California wine country, a 100 year old log cabin in the Adirondacks, and a flat in London overlooking the Thames.

For a complete listing of books, as well as excerpts and contests, and to connect with Bella:

**Sign up for Bella's newsletter:**
**BellaAndre.com/Newsletter**

**Visit Bella's website at:**
**www.BellaAndre.com**

**Follow Bella on Twitter at:**
**twitter.com/bellaandre**

**Join Bella on Facebook at:**
**facebook.com/bellaandrefans**

**Follow Bella on Instagram:**
**instagram.com/bellaandrebooks**

Made in the USA
Lexington, KY
28 June 2019